CHINA
'SPY'

GEORGE WATT

DIANE BOOKS　　　　GLENDALE, CALIFORNIA

First United States Printing 1973

CONTENTS

Chapter		Page
I	Boyhood in Ulster	7
II	Nigeria and Ghana	17
III	Russia and Ukraine	29
IV	Assignment China	44
V	Lanchow: The Atomic City	48
VI	Our First Contretemps	56
VII	The Cultural Revolution	65
VIII	My Wife's Visit	74
IX	The Sacking of the Peking Mission	88
X	Alone in Peking	98
XI	Return to Lanchow	108
XII	I Confess	118
XIII	The Ideological Remolding Prison	124
Appendix III		
	Brainwashing	141
Appendix II		
	Businessmen in China	148
Appendix I		
	Extract from Hansard	155

ACKNOWLEDGEMENTS

Acknowledgements are due for their help in publishing this account of my story to the following:

Mrs. Slava Stetsko
Professor Wolhodymyr Shayan
Petro Mykytiuk
Charles C. S. Wang
Shen Shan
Colin Neil MacKay
Dean Clarence E. Manion
Senator Peter Dominick
Lee Edwards
Hugh Newton

and my publisher, Dr. Donald McI. Johnson.

The Controller of Her Majesty's Stationery Office for the permission to reproduce the page of *Hansard* of 13th June, 1968.

I would also like to acknowledge several others who cannot be named as they are not at present in the Free World.

GEORGE WATT

AUTHOR'S FOREWORD

I can still feel the chill of the Chinese wind that blew in through the open windows of the town hall in Lanchow.

I was ordered to stand on a platform similar to those used to acclaim triumphant Olympic athletes. The hall was packed with hundreds of Chinese men and women, some of them no older than teenagers. All were yelling and pointing at me. I could almost feel the hatred.

From the floor, an interpreter shouted again and again and again:

"Bow your head, George Watt. Bow to the masses."

In front of me sat my Chinese judge. No bearded sage in wig and scarlet robes, but a woman. She was small, with what appeared to be a good figure, even in loose uniform. She couldn't have been much more than 21 or 22. I remember thinking that she might even have passed as attractive—if her face had not been so twisted with revulsion and rage. Against me.

Behind her chair was an enormous blow-up picture of Mao Tse-tung. They made an incongruous couple. If the situation hadn't been so serious, it might have been a scene right out of a Hollywood "B" picture with Peter Lorre and Sidney Greenstreet.

For nearly an hour she had been screaming at me. Now she spat—not for the first time—straight in my face, and yelled:

"George Watt, you are an Imperialist spy. . . . In view of the Chinese policy of leniency towards those who admit their crimes, you will receive the extremely lenient penalty of three years' imprisonment; for you have told the truth."

The crowd roared. One couldn't be certain, but they sounded hysterical with frustration. My interpreter, who was never far from my side, said in my ear—and with obvious relish:

"They are not happy that you are getting off so lightly. The masses are calling for your blood."

I stayed with my head bowed. With my right hand, I shielded my eyes in what I hoped was a gesture of true penitence. Through slightly parted fingers I stared at the swaying, yelling mob, and I recall saying to myself:

"Those people are mad. Really mad. These Chinese Communists are absolutely bloody raving mad."

And on that platform, on that freezing March morning in 1968, I swore that if ever I got out alive from Red China, I'd tell the world the truth.

GEORGE WATT

Cheltenham
1972

CHAPTER I

Boyhood in Ulster

I am Irish—and proud of it—and, as my name implies, I am also of Scottish descent.

But let me add quickly that I do not belong to the Ireland from which the Kennedy Clan emanates.

I was born in Belfast, Northern, Ireland; I am an Ulsterman.

Ulster, with its 5,462 square miles, is only a third of the size of Switzerland. It has a population of only 1,500,000, which is not much more than that of Glasgow or Birmingham.

There are no precise census figures. But in percentage terms the population is reckoned to be 34.9 per cent Roman Catholic, 29 per cent Presbyterian, 24.2 per cent Church of Ireland, 5 per cent Methodist, 4.9 per cent "others", and 2 per cent not stated.

I have no wish to indulge in religious or racial discrimination, but it is important to set the record straight, particularly at the present juncture, when facts may so easily be distorted. To ensure that the premises in this book are well founded let me emphasize right away that Ulster is much more than a geographical term.

Ulster is not merely another way of saying "Northern Ireland". Ulster constitutes a way of life and a way of worship. It means, too, an almost fanatical devotion and loyalty to the British Crown.

An Ulsterman is staunchly patriotic, and in our Protestant faith we are, if anything, more passionately Presbyterian than the Moderator of the General Assembly of the Church of Scotland.

Although, historically, Ulster was one of the four Irish provinces, the name has become a convenient synonym for the somewhat smaller governmental area of Northern Ireland.

The name Northern Ireland is to be found in history and geography books only since the year 1920.

But it represents the continuation of an old political entity rather than the creation of a new one, for it is the part of Ireland which opted to remain within the United Kingdom when the rest of the island seceded to become the Irish Free State—now the Irish Republic.

Before 1920 Ireland as a whole formed part of the United Kingdom. It was then termed The United Kingdom of Great Britain and Ireland, whereas it is now "of Great Britain and *Northern Ireland*".

But although, geographically and politically, Ireland was then one country, racially it was composed of two distinct groups who, except in trade and commerce, remained separate.

In the years before 1920, the desire for a measure of Home Rule—which ultimately developed into a demand for complete separation from the United Kingdom—had been gaining in strength among one of those groups.

This movement was resisted by the other group who, in addition to having close racial and religious affinities with Great Britain, believed that the United Kingdom and Ireland formed a natural political and economic entity, and hence were determined that things should remain that way. The Unionists—as they came to be known—amounted to about a quarter of the population. They were largely composed of descendants of Scottish and English settlers, and were mostly of Protestant faith. They had, therefore, close racial and religious ties with Great Britain.

On the other hand, the group among whom the breakaway movement was developing—the Home Rulers were mostly descended from the early Celtic settlers in Ireland, and were largely of Roman Catholic faith. Thus the division by religion was identical with the racial division. Because of the strong religious convictions held by both of these groups, there was little assimilation between them down the years.

Religious differences also entered into the Unionist-Home Rule controversy of the late nineteenth and early twentieth century. The Roman Catholic Home Rulers

8

found themselves in spiritual disagreement with Protestant Britain. The Unionist descendants of the Protestant British, who over the centuries had settled in Ireland, were apprehensive that Home Rule would result in the setting up of a state which would be dominated by a religion alien to them.

Although there were a number of Unionists in Southern Ireland, mostly among the landed and professional classes, the group was concentrated mainly in the northern province of Ulster; particularly in the north-east, where many Scots had settled about the end of the sixteenth century. In this they were, in a sense, returning to their native shore, for it was the "Scots" from the north-east of Ulster who, from the third century, had invaded the land of the Picts, to which they eventually gave the name of Scotland.

But during the intervening period the language and culture of these "returning" people had undergone extensive changes, due to the Anglo-Norman influence, whilst the Reformation had had a profound effect on their religious beliefs.

The number of Protestants in Ireland was further increased during the reign of King James VI of Scotland (who, on the death of Queen Elizabth in 1603, became James I of England). Following the defeat and flight to the Continent of the principal Celtic chiefs in Ulster who had been waging war against Elizabeth, King James, in the second decade of the seventeenth century, introduced large numbers of Scottish and English settlers to the lands which the defeated chiefs had forfeited.

The land we now call Northern Ireland thus came to be peopled largely by these settlers and their descendants, and things have remained that way to this day. Because of the proximity to Scotland, the Scottish influence proved to be the dominant one, although the people of Northern Ireland also inherited many of the characteristics of the English settlers.

A homogeneous community developed, distinctively British in culture. With the accession to the throne of William of Orange the people were deeply loyal to the Sovereign, and they remained Protestant by religion. It is to these days

9

and to these traditions that we can trace the origins of the powerful Orange Lodges, which still exist.

The fact that the settlers were industrious by nature and sturdily independent in outlook enabled them to survive the difficulties and dangers which beset them in their early years in Ulster. During the course of their first century they played a decisive part in the shaping of history, for at Enniskillen, Londonderry, and in the Battle of the Boyne, 12 July, 1690, they became the pivot of the successful struggle of Britain and her European allies against Louis XIV of France to prevent a Jacobite restoration in England —and the consequent domination of the world by the French Monarchy.

Even then—nearly three centuries ago—the struggle was between two racial and religious groups in Ireland whose descendants finally parted company in 1920. Seen in this light, it is understandable that the anniversary of the Battle of the Boyne has been celebrated in Ulster ever since.

An Ulsterman such as myself is sustained in life by twin faiths—basic, unshakable belief in Christianity, and fervid allegiance to the British Monarchy.

This is the atmosphere into which I was born and grew up in the city of Belfast. . . .

Little did I realize at the time how valuable this indoctrination would later prove in my fight against Communism.

It is perhaps difficult for anyone who doesn't know Northern Ireland to realize how strong this patriotic feeling is. Our dedication to the Monarchy and to Protestantism transcends everything—class, background, education. And we support the Ulster Unionist Party which is pro-British and one hundred per cent Conservative.

In this maze of interlocking religious and political beliefs, the youth of Northern Ireland are reared. It is a whirlwind pattern that can defy rational thinking. Although my own views have broadened and mellowed as I have got older, and in spite of my travels across the world, I have never been able to disregard completely my early training.

*   *   *

As I mentioned earlier, there is a close affiliation between the people of Northern Ireland and the Scots—much closer than between Ulster and Eire.

My own family, centuries ago, arrived from Scotland, and founded a little township in County Londonderry which they called Bally Watt—*Bally* being Gaelic for "Town of".

Generations later, they moved into the market town of Coleraine. My parents remained there until a few days before my birth, when they set up house in the capital city of Belfast.

Belfast was then, and still is, a grimy bustling town where the people live almost on the factory doorsteps. It was in the narrow streets of this industrial center that I grew up.

I was born and lived the early part of my life in East Belfast, in Templemore Avenue, on the edge of a working class district. My mother died when I was only two years old and for a time my grandmother took over the task of looking after the family. Then my father remarried—my mother's younger sister, whom I have always known affectionately as Aunt Lily, and shortly after this event we moved to another part of Belfast, a residential, suburban area.

At school I was a mischievous adventurous type of child, always climbing into places where I should not climb, going places where I should not go, and as a result getting into all sorts of predicaments.

My companions nicknamed me "Vandal", because I tended to wreck everything I touched. Even now, when I go back home on a visit, they say, "And how is George Vandal?"

At the time though I wasn't quite sure what "vandal" meant, and I admit to being rather horrified to find that my dictionary defined it as "one of a fierce people who passed from north-eastern Germany to Gaul, Spain, and North Africa—and sacked Rome in 455, destroying Catholic churches".

I must say, in answer to that, that although I got up to all kinds of high jinks in Soviet Russia and Red China, I regard religious freedom as one of man's basic rights, and would never myself discriminate against a member of any church or religion.

I was still a child during the grim, hungry years of the late 1930's and at this time of soaring unemployment we looked on my father, a construction foreman, as someone who had reached the pinnacle of success—for he managed to keep his job though the male members of almost every family we knew in Ulster had been thrown out of work.

About this time, at the age of nine or ten, I had my first introduction to Ulster politics. . . . I remember standing at a street corner, surrounded by working men and "shawlies"—women who wore woollen shawls around their heads and over their shoulders in accordance with local custom.

It was election time. The contenders were the pro-British Ulster Unionist and a Socialist—or, as we then called them, the Labour Party.

One knows that conditions of economic depression are more favorable to the Socialists; the extreme Left-wingers and the Communists seem to thrive on the misery of others. At their meetings they love to gloat and repeat in parrot fashion, "We told you it was too good to last, but you wouldn't believe us."

It followed, therefore, that Ulster, with its high rate of unemployment, would support the Labour candidate.

Instead, the reverse happened.

I can see now the Unionist candidates arriving on lorries, every available inch bedecked with Union Jacks, and with bands playing patriotic tunes. At the end of the meetings, everyone would stand to attention, fingers down the seams of trousers, and sing the National Anthem.

On the other hand, the Labour candidates provided little entertainment. To their disadvantage, they seemed to be interested only in putting across a political message. No music, no Union Jacks and to add insult to injury, they never played *God Save the King* at the end. Disappointing —and, to our juvenile minds, a drab performance.

*   *   *

In those early days, so far as the people were concerned, it was not a matter of policy; not a question of which political party had the most to offer. It was simply and starkly this. . . . The Ulster Unionists played the National Anthem and waved the Union Jack. The Labour Party did not.

Who, therefore, in their right senses would vote for the Labour candidates? How could they? *They were not British.*

Although more than ten years have passed since I left Ireland, and I have travelled throughout the world, I still can't shake off the old beliefs molded in my Ulster childhood.

I am still of the opinion that if the Devil himself and his disciples should enter the elections in Northern Ireland, they would be assured of seats in the House of Commons—provided they played the National Anthem and remembered to wave the Union Jack.

In Ireland, it was the practice for most people who had not the opportunity to go to college or university to leave school at fourteen, and go into local industry—which in Belfast inevitably meant the shipyards.

My father decided, although he could barely afford it, to send me to technical college in the neighboring town of Lisburn. This gave me the advantage of a two-year preapprenticeship engineering course.

I dearly enjoyed those two years, and was filled with ambition now for a university career.

Alas, those were still the days before widespread educational grants and the family finances wouldn't stretch that far. So I began a proper apprenticeship and knuckled down to some really hard work, in the world-famous shipbuilding yard at Harland and Wolff in Belfast.

This was a great moment in my life. I reasoned that with the two years of technical training behind me, I'd go straight into the office—a spick-and-span white collar worker—and sit at a drawing board.

So on Monday morning I collected my slide rule and compasses, and presented myself before the General Foreman. He stared at me, perhaps not with distaste, but certainly not with the welcoming smile appropriate for a

13

budding genius. He said slowly, "And just what do you think you're going to do?" There were a dozen or so apprentices milling around, pretending to be busy, but in reality all ears. They looked grubby and unwashed, so I immediately discounted them.

Jauntily, I pointed out to the General Foreman that, as I had acquired at least a veneer of education, he wasn't going to waste my talents on manual work. A boss with such perspicacity as he possessed would without a doubt start me off a few rungs up the ladder.

At this point I was ignorant of two attributes of the General Foreman. First, in that shipyard, he had absolute authority and, secondly, he didn't waste words.

His answer was, "We'll see."

My hopes soared; disciplinarian he might be, but this man clearly recognized my superior brains and skill.

He turned me over to one of the under-foremen, and in a matter of minutes Watt the engineering genius was carrying out duties appropriate to his status. I was given a wire brush, and told to clean out soot from an old boiler. He told me to be sharp about it, because when I had finished I could have the honor of making everyone some tea.

So much for my technical education—when I got home that night, I looked like a chimney sweep. Looking back, though, I suppose that day taught me a salutary lesson.

* * *

The only thing I didn't like about my apprenticeship was the feeling of being imprisoned. I rebelled against the idea of having to clock into a yard or a factory on the minute, leave when the hooter sounded, and have a regimented life in between. I didn't want to spend the rest of my days standing at a work-bench, making profits for others.

But the question was, what could I do about it? It was indeed a big question for a sixteen-year-old who hardly had enough money in his pocket to pay his bus fare to work.

It was a challenge; but I recall feeling even then that the

14

bigger the challenge, the greater the satisfaction when one overcomes it. I looked at my fellow apprentices. They had resigned themselves to their fate. They would marry one of the local mill girls—usually referred to as "a smashing bit of stuff"—live in a matchbox house in a Belfast tenement, and have endless children.

I saw a way out. I decided that I should have to use my smattering of education, and build upon it. Although I was a mechanical engineer during the day, in the world of steel, I would be in the world of *construction* in the evenings.

My mind made up, I straight away enrolled for night classes in the building department of the Belfast College of Advanced Technology. And this became the pattern of my life, finish work during the day and walk straight into the technical college for a full evening's study.

I had neither time nor money for cinemas, theatres, dancing or girls. My only recreations were junior football at weekends, and occasional sessions with sparring partners at a boxing club.

After twelve months things became easier for a time when I obtained a scholarship which allowed me to leave my daytime apprenticeship, and take a full-time course.

I continued to study, both on a part-time and on a full-time basis as circumstances permitted, until I had completed my apprenticeship and obtained my qualifications. Then came the great day when I walked up to the foreman at Harland and Wolff's and said, as laconically as I could— although I was consumed with nerves—"I'm leaving tonight. I want my cards."

That evening I packed all my tools into their box and walked on air up the Queen's Road. I have never looked back. The very next day I started at the College of Advanced Technology.

I did some part-time teaching, mostly to apprentices in the evenings, and, as I had spare time during the day, I opened a small building business and carried out subcontract work for building contractors, mainly plumbing and central heating. I employed a small gang of workmen, and was able to operate on a competitive basis.

In next to no time I was able to put down a deposit on a second-hand truck. But on the price I put on my little contracts, I had to work extremely hard to make ends meet and I was hard at it for sixteen hours a day.

There was, however, another reason for my needing to make money; I was in love, and wanted to get married.

The lady was Josephine Angela Davis, my childhood sweetheart. We had first met when her father, an officer in the Royal Air Force, was posted to Belfast. It was a whirlwind romance, a love story straight out of a Victorian novel. Jo was only sixteen and her parents wanted her to wait until she was twenty one. In deference to her family, we waited; and on 24 February, 1956, we were married in Belmont Presbyterian Church, Belfast.

We moved into our new house, in which I'd installed the plumbing and central heating as a private arrangement in lieu of putting down a deposit.

It certainly wasn't a bed of roses for Jo; I was slaving so hard that she seldom saw me, except at weekends.

Finally, I decided that it was time for a change; I had become just a slave to work, and I wanted to do something different. So one night early in 1960 when Jo was asleep I got out my old school atlas. I quickly flipped the map of Ireland out of the way; the first thing to do was to get out of Ulster. Suddenly I found myself looking at a map of West Africa—there was Nigeria which, together with the Gold Coast (now, of course, Ghana) I had known as "the White Man's Grave".

That seemed to be challenge enough. As it appeared to be the last place on earth that anyone would want to go, I decided that Nigeria would be my first.

When I told Jo next morning what I planned, I knew immediately that I didn't really have to discuss it with her. She is one of those women in a million who will back her husband one hundred per cent. If I had announced that I was going to the Moon, she'd say, "Fine, I'm coming with you."

And so Jo and I—with our infant daughter, Christine—prepared for the big adventure. Within weeks, I was successful in being appointed by the Crown Agents to go to Nigeria as a Government officer on technical education.

CHAPTER II
Nigeria and Ghana

Jo and I sold up our home in Belfast, put our furniture into store, and embarked on the first stage of our journey to West Africa—the Belfast ferry to Liverpool.

I had never previously been outside Northern Ireland or, indeed, further than my native Coleraine, and I'll never forget the sensation of standing on deck, looking over the rail. For the first time in my life I was crossing the Irish Sea, going away from Ireland.

I gazed down at the crowd on the quayside, a scene I was to witness many times afterwards. It is a situation always highly charged with emotion; emigrants are leaving home and loved ones, many knowing that this is the last time, and that they will never return. It is difficult to realize that this scene is faithfully re-enacted every night; the same play, with a different cast.

The participants go through a fixed performance. The ever-present Salvation Army band plays hymns from the Moody and Sankey[1] collection. The favorites in my day were *Gather with the saints at the river that flows by the Throne of God* and *In the sweet by-and-by, we shall meet on that beautiful shore.*

Then as the call goes out over the loud speakers, "All ashore that's going ashore", the pattern changes—and the music.

Auld Lang Syne is announced. Everyone links hands and sings—a least that is the theory. It will be appreciated that this can be a tricky operation, when you are grasping a tumblerful of Old Bushmills whiskey in one hand, and wiping away maudlin tears with the other.

---

[1] Dwight Lyman Moody (1837-99), American revivalist preacher, associated on both sides of the Atlantic in mission work with Ira D. Sankey, 'the American Singing Pilgrim' (1840-1908).

The singing is cut short by peremptory blasts on the ship's siren. Lines are let go fore and aft. In a sudden silence they splash into the black, scummy water, like so many bodies sewn in sackcloth. Then, as the propellers churn yellow foam, the ship edges from the quay. And across the ever-widening gap that many of us will never bridge again, there comes incredibly the words of *Will Ye No' Come Back Again?*

Incredible from a Salvation Army band and the loyal throats of Ulstermen.

Over the thrum of the screws, as the ship points her bows eastwards for England—the words drift across from the shore:

> Better lo'ed ye canna be,
> Will ye no' come back again?

Incredible, because they are the words of a Jacobite air, composed by Lady Nairne (1766-1845). The title, *Bonnie Charlie's Noo Awa'* is a lament for the departure of Prince Charles Edward Stuart, the Young Pretender—Bonnie Prince Charlie.

I couldn't help thinking that if the "bonnie" prince hadn't been defeated and driven into exile there wouldn't be a Protestant Ulster, or a Protestant Queen on the British Throne.

But as the short lights were swallowed up by the darkness, I suddenly saw the funny side. Only the Irish could sing a Jacobite song, and not know it. Or not care . . .

*   *   *

Our adventure really began at Liverpool when we boarded the Elder Dempster line ship, *Apapa*, which was to be our home for the fourteen-day voyage to Lagos, Federal capital of Nigeria.

The date was April, 1960.

A few weeks before, Mr. Harold Macmillan had made his famous "wind of change" speech to the South African Parliament. President de Gaulle was on a State visit to Britain.

But the Watt family were not concerned with world af-

18

fairs. Until we were clear of the Bay of Biscay, Jo, I, and the baby were confined to our quarters—seasick. An unnerving experience.

But as we moved along the West African coast, the weather improved. Then one day it was quite hot and the swimming pools on the ship were suddenly filled with people.

I was fascinated to mingle with people who had been to West Africa before; they proudly referred to themselves as "old coasters".

I remember having drinks with one old character who insisted that there was "a magic" about Africa which always draws the white man back. But I didn't realize then the truth of his words. How quickly I was to discover that Africa is indeed a continent of mystery.

As we sailed down the coast the smell of decayed vegetation was carried out by the offshore winds. And the old coasters would pronounce solemnly, "That is Africa. We must be getting close now."

Our first port of call, Bathurst in Gambia, was exciting. The native traders came out in boats and swarmed on board offering trinkets and carved ivories for sale—all for a ridiculously high price.

Then south to Freetown, the beautiful capital of Sierra Leone, and on to Takoradi, the then port for Ghana. And finally to our goal—Lagos.

On these stops along the coast I first heard what is known as the great call of Africa—"Dash me, master." I was mystified by this, until an old colonial explained that "dash" is a gift, and nothing happens in commerce until a "dash" or a bribe is involved. This inbred system of "dash" leads to a tremendous amount of corruption among the Africans.

Whenever a contract is negotiated, there is always an extra added for "dashing". Even when a domestic servant such as a cook employs a garden boy, the boy would have to "dash" half his wages before getting the job. Nobody will do anything without receiving a dash.

At Lagos we were picked up by a truck, and driven a hundred miles along red dusty roads inland to the capital of the Western Region, Ibadan; a town of about 600,000 people—a little bigger than Scotland's capital, Edinburgh.

We spent the first night in what they were pleased to call a Government "rest house". This was a type of primitive hotel. We didn't get a wink of sleep all night; enormous spiders crawled in from every available opening in the walls—and there were plenty. They were soon joined by battalions of lizards, flopping on top of the sagging mosquito nets over our beds, their sharp claws tearing at the mesh. What an initiation poor Jo had into the glories of West Africa!

In the morning, unslept, stiff, bleary-eyed, but still full of enthusiasm, I hurried round to the Government offices to see my prospective boss, the Chief Technical Education Officer. After the usual preliminaries, during which he made light of our nocturnal horrors, I said how much I was looking forward to beginning duties at the technical college.

He stared at me. Then, unaccountably, he burst out laughing.

Annoyed that I couldn't see the joke, I tried to assume an air of what I hoped was polite bewilderment.

"You are now", he said, "in West Africa. In this part of the world things seldom go as planned. For your information, there is no technical college. We haven't even started building it yet. We are, however, about to prepare construction plans. If all goes well it should be completed in a few years from now."

I couldn't say a word, but my face must have spoken volumes.

Patting me on the shoulder, he said in a kindly, reassuring voice, "Don't worry. In the meantime, we'll find some other duties for you."

And so it was decided—as a temporary measure—that I should be attached to the staff of a Government Trade Centre. This was several hundred miles eastwards, over duty tracks and rickety wooden bridges, at the inland port of Sapele, on the upper reaches of a navigable river, the Ethiope. Sapele was a familiar name to me, as a splendid type of mahogany is grown in the area, known the world over as Sapele.

The vegetation in this region, with its humid climate, is luxuriant, but there were certainly less pleasant aspects of life here. There were the swarms of sandflies, and crocodiles were no unusual sight in the River Ethiope. Indeed I was horrified to hear that just about the time I arrived at the Government Trade Centre a party of some twenty boys had gone to bathe, to return a few hours later short of one member of the original party!

But the various tropical diseases common to this part of the world provide an even greater menace to the population than do the crocodiles. Particularly devastating are malaria, elephantiasis and a disease which affects the liver, bilharzia.

I felt really sorry for Jo when we saw our living quarters. There was no running water, no electricity, and no facilities at all for cooking even the simplest meal. I knew she was already regretting leaving the little house in Belfast—though it was hard to believe that we had left just over two weeks before.

As the next day was Sunday we decided to go to church. This meant a drive across country to Sapele, to the little Presbyterian church.

After the service we took a short cut through the cemetery to pick up some provisions in the market.

I stopped again and again at the tombstones. So many of them bore English names; usually hyphenated names—pioneers of the British Empire who had served their country as district commissioners.

But what brought me up sharply was that, in some cases, it was indicated that they had died after being in West Africa only a year or even less—clearly they had been victims of malaria and other tropical diseases. I remember reflecting on that Sabbath morning what a magnificent spirit imbued those heroes—for heroes they were, however unsung. They carried on unflaggingly, knowing that the graveyard awaited them, in those days before modern treatments had been developed. It was a moving sight.

Jo looked white and shaken. As we reached the gates, she stopped and looked me in the eye. I'll always remember her words. She said steadily, without recrimination, without rancor—because these are not in her nature—"Well, George, you've got your wish. We are certainly in the White Man's Grave."

Guiltily, I thought how glamorous and daring that phrase had sounded back home in Belfast. Suddenly it took on a grim significance. As I looked back on the mounds that covered the bones of those trailblazers for Britain, I wondered how foolish I had been in bringing my wife and our infant daughter.

*   *   *

We both accepted the circumstances as philosophically as we could. My attitude was then, and is now, "One dies without worrying—and much quicker by worrying. So—why worry?"

As I was then surplus to establishment at the Government Trade Centre, I was looked on as a kind of odd-job man, and detailed to supervise various construction projects.

My first reaction was that West Africa was really going to boom, because labor was so very, very cheap. It would clearly be a magnet for investors. So the standard of living would increase correspondingly. This was my glorious theory. In practice, however, it didn't work that way.

I put some laborers on to excavating a trench for a pipe-line. The ground was soft and sandy, unlike the heavy thick clay that I was accustomed to in Ireland. At the end of the day I calculated the exact volume of earth excavated, and the wages for the job.

I had in my luggage an old accounts book for similar work done at home. I got a shock when I compared the figures, and a salutary lesson in practical economics. The work in West Africa was many times more expensive than a similar operation in the United Kingdom.

It then dawned on me that, although the wages were appallingly low, the amount of work which one got in return was lower still. What at first glance appeared to be cheap labor was, in fact, very expensive.

My figures proved, at least to my personal satisfaction, that one Irish laborer—or navvy—could produce more work than twelve Nigerian natives.

It seemed to me that this was a simple demonstration why the tropics will never be the home of heavy industry.

＊　　＊　　＊

As a family, we soon settled in. Even our complexions soon changed from lobster pink to—at least with Jo and Christine—an attractive light brown tan.

The weeks passed lazily, and then, in mid-1960, an election was held to decide the government for the new Independent Nigeria, before independence was obtained on 1 October.

My expatriate colleagues and myself were detailed to look after the administration of the elections. Each was allocated a constituency, to ensure that the voting followed the line of accepted British democracy. I was given a "centre", which amounted to nothing more than a sizeable village deep in the jungle, north of Sapele.

So I, a greenhorn officer, set off with my checkers and porters several days before the election. After a few miles by car, the road disappeared, and we followed barely discernible tracks on foot, the beaters going ahead with machetes, a sword-like knife, cutting away the undergrowth. Eventually, many footsore miles and thousands of mosquito-bites later, we arrived at my temporary headquarters—a large hut in the centre of a native village.

There were two opposing parties, both of which were in favor of independence with slight differences. As most of the West Africans were completely illiterate, it was decided that the parties would adopt symbols—so the Action Group used the symbol of a palm tree, and the other party, the Nigerian Congress Party, a hen.

As the day wore on two huge queues formed outside the polling station, men on one side, women on the other.

I didn't interfere, but allowed them to file in to cast their votes. All the same, the thought kept nagging me as to why there should be two queues; was this some kind of sex discrimination? Vaguely, I suppose, I associated it with the practice in Northern Ireland, where women don't go into the public bar. I assumed that in this part of Nigeria women didn't use the same door of a public building as their men folk.

It didn't seem too important anyway, and as I watched the scene I felt happy that these people were now—so I thought—deciding their own future.

But it turned out that I couldn't have been more mistaken.

I explained earlier that Africans in the main are absolutely corrupt—and what was happening in this "democratic" election was as follows. . . .

The candidate represented by the palm tree was offering as a bribe—or the traditional "dash"—drinks of fresh palm wine; a most acceptable offer to the men. His opponent, represented by the hen, offered eggs in return for votes—just what the thrifty housewife needed.

In my particular constituency, as there were more eligible men than women, they carried the day.

When the election was over, I submitted a report on what I considered to be a monstrous irregularity; not surprisingly, nothing developed.

We declared "Mr. Palm Tree" elected, and I returned to my quarters on the outskirts of Sapele.

I mentioned the incident to some of my colleagues. They had different stories to tell. One said that the electors in his constituency didn't follow such undemocratic practices. The chiefs just marched in at the head of their villagers, and entered the polling booths with them. Each chief made sure that the members of his particular village voted according to *his* wishes. The chief then received payment from the candidate concerned, and marched them all back to his outlying village. Clean, tidy, uncomplicated, and "most democratic".

Another officer complained that, when he was returning after the election with the ballot boxes, he was waylaid on a river bank by canoe-loads of grinning Africans—not aggressive in the least, but quite good-natured, as they usually are. But they impounded his ballot boxes for a while for what they termed "a pre-count count". They returned them to him in due course and sent him on his way.

*   *   *

My years in Nigeria were crammed with exciting and fascinating detail; but this book is not the place for them.

By 1964, the technical college to which I had originally been posted, was finally completed. It was under the sponsorship of the University of Michigan, U.S.A. I was transferred to the staff and spent many happy months there before deciding that I'd had enough of Nigeria. Jo and myself were longing for a spell at home in the United Kingdom.

As a contract officer I could easily have opted for another tour of duty. But I could see—only too clearly—the writing on the wall.

The various expatriate officers, both in Government and commercial interests, were leaving at speed. The country had a policy of "nativization", which resulted in chaos.

So, in August 1964, we embarked on the trip home.

In any case Christine was now of school age, and I have always felt that children shouldn't be carted around the world like so much baggage.

We decided to make our headquarters in England, and chose Cheltenham, that beautiful town on the edge of the Cotswolds, famous for its health-giving mineral waters. I must admit, though, as a rough Ulsterman, I was a little apprehensive about our reception; for Cheltenham had always been the butt of music-hall jokes. It was regarded, not incorrectly, as a retirement place for retired Army officers and elderly widows. I was certain that there wouldn't be a pub in the place, let alone a billiards saloon or—perish the thought—a boxing booth.

I was wrong. The people of Cheltenham took us to their hearts, and we still live there.

I must emphasize that although I am very much a family man and have no desire to be parted from my wife and children, I realize that I can earn more money for them as an engineer by working abroad, especially in places

25

where most people are reluctant to go. I've often thought that I might so easily have become one of the hapless unemployed in Belfast, shuffling around street corners, and so have entered the "Demand your rights" gang. But I'm all for peddling my own canoe.

For a while I went to work in London, in a building company in Wimbledon—a hundred miles from Cheltenham by road. But I couldn't settle in the noise and general pollution and above all I hated being tied to an office from nine till five.

So I made up my mind to make one more trip—just one—back to the Africa which I had found so attractive and compelling.

This time, however, instead of teaching construction, I would participate in it.

Within a few months I had got a job with an American construction company, the Kaiser Engineering Company, as a senior construction general foreman on the Bauxite Smelter plant on the Volta River project at Tema—the new harbor town near Accra, capital of Ghana.

I've always liked working with Americans; they are so industrious. On the other hand, they certainly like to have their comforts. Once, when the air conditioning broke down, we had groups of Americans lined up outside, complaining that they must be flown home on compassionate grounds. No white man, they contended, could possibly survive in such conditions. I refrained from pointing out that I had lived for four years in Nigeria without any air conditioning—and I survived all right.

I should, however, like to place on record that I really did enjoy American construction methods. I thought that, with my practical and technical background, I was no fool, and knew most of the answers. In fact, I learned an enormous amount from the Americans, and found the experience simply fascinating.

Ghana, formerly the Gold Coast, is only a quarter of the size of Nigeria, with about eight million people against Nigeria's 55 million.

In the years under the Socialist dictatorship of Dr. Kwame Nkrumah, "the Redeemer", the rot had obviously set in, and when I arrived in Ghana corruption was everywhere. It was, for example, virtually impossible to buy consumer goods in the shops. Most expatriates managed to arrange for their salaries to be paid in hard currency. It was said that Ghanaian currency was at par with most international currencies; in other words, that a British £ was equal to a Ghanaian £. If you changed a British pound note at the bank, you'd be given a Ghanaian one. But this was strictly one-way traffic. If you had a wad of Ghanaian notes, you soon found that it was impossible to get British notes in return, or American dollars, or, indeed, any other hard currency. This, of course, led to tremendous abuse, and to a black market which everyone knew about. The unofficial rate of exchange was three Ghanaian pounds to one British pound.

The unofficial bankers were mainly Lebanese traders, who had a near-monopoly in the night clubs of Accra.

Expatriates could apply to the Ghanaian government for what was called a "personal remittance quota". This meant that part of their wages could be returned, at par level, to their country of origin. In other cases it worked out at only a third of any salary which they actually earned in Ghanaian currency.

Let us say, for example, you were permitted to refund under personal remittance quo t the sum of £180. All you had to do was write a check on your British bank for £60 in hard cash. You then took it along to a Lebanese trader, who would give you a rate of three to one. So you now had £180 in Ghanaian currency. You could then deposit it at the Government bank and have it remitted home in hard currency.

I recall one day being called to a meeting with a senior Ghanaian (black) official. He was a high ranking officer in the Special Branch, whose mission was to eliminate corruption, and he warned us solemnly not to participate in any way in illicit currency dealings. It was fear-inspiring to hear him reel off the dire penalties for so doing.

Some of my colleagues were whispering among themselves, "That's him; that's him all right." I wondered what on earth was going on.

Soon afterwards I was sitting with a companion in one of the bungalows when this same Ghanaian official arrived and began collecting checks. He was quite openly paying out three times the amount in Ghanaian money.

I said to him tentatively, "Surely you're the man who was giving us an official lecture today against illicit practices, and here you are dabbling in it yourself?"

He looked utterly bland and unconcerned.

"Yes, that is so. But it is now after working hours. When I spoke to you earlier, it was in my official capacity. Tonight I am operating in my private business capacity. You see, there is quite a difference."

He smiled, and there appeared to be no hint of guilt. I was so stunned, I just sat there without saying a word.

This was typical of the topsy-turvy world of Ghana.

The entire population was disciplined into worshipping Nkrumah, and I would stand watching school children marching to their lessons, all carrying banners adorned with Nkrumah's picture, surrounded by inscriptions of all the wonderful titles he had bestowed on himself.

This was a strictly regimented population, most unlike the Nigerians I had left only months before. I was certainly not impressed by this enforced Socialism which Nkrumah backed up by his Special Branch. He was billed as the greatest of African leaders, and as he was convinced that the people weren't intelligent enough to know not to vote for any party but his own, he took the precaution of adopting a one-party system.

*   *   *

My profession is also my hobby. I became completely engrossed by my work in Ghana, and I would sometimes return to the site in the evenings. I would always be first on parade in the morning, too. Eventually, this was noticed by my superiors and very soon, I was promoted to be a Department Manager.

I ended a complete tour of duty with that company and returned home to Jo, Christine and year-old infant son Steven in Cheltenham early in 1966.

As a final note on my years in Africa, I should like to say that it has always been my firm belief that to acquire accurate information about a country it is necessary to live there and participate in the life and work of the people—not on a package-deal holiday, but over a lengthy period of time.

My many years of living and travelling in African countries have convinced me that, on the whole, the African people have not been able to demonstrate beyond reasonable doubt that they possess the ability to rule themselves.

No doubt many well-meaning—but untravelled—do-gooders will scream, "One man, one vote". On the surface this appears to be morally just. But my personal opinion is that democracy as we know it in the free world is a luxury—which the masses of happy-go-lucky, child-like, Africans have not yet been developed to participate in and enjoy.

In this there lies the tragedy of the African peoples for, with the departure of the old colonial powers from the African continent, a vacuum has been created, which the Chinese and the Russians are only too ready to fill. Incapable as they are as yet of setting up western-style democracies, the African nations have left themselves wide open to Communist infiltration.

CHAPTER III

Russia and Ukraine

Back in Britain after six years in West Africa, I looked around for work. I soon had three firm offers, ranging from Canada to the Congo and the Persian Gulf.

I was still trying to decide which one to accept when suddenly, completely out of the blue, came a request to attend an interview with an Anglo-German company, Vickers-Zimmer, a member of the famous Vickers Group, manufacturers of munitions in both World Wars.

Vickers-Zimmer, of course, specialize in the petrochemical field, mainly in building plants to produce synthetic fibres in overseas countries.

I was offered the post of Resident Site Engineer on a project soon to begin in Red China—in Lanchow, in the province of Kansu.

Since it was common knowledge that it took months to obtain a visa, and I couldn't afford to hang around the London office kicking my heels, I was posted on a temporary basis to a nylon plant in Ukraine.

I remember how excited I was at the prospect of working in Ukraine. The Ukranian Soviet Socialist Republic.

A constituent republic in the south-west of the Soviet Union, Ukraine is about the same size as France, with a population estimated to be about 50,000,000 people.

A flat and fertile land with rich black earth, Ukraine is still predominantly agricultural, producing 60 per cent of all sugar requirements of the Soviet Union. But today the economy of Ukraine is a mixed one and it is becoming more and more industrialized; it is now the main center of Soviet coal mining and of the Soviet iron and steel industry. In 1955 Ukraine provided 37 per cent of all Soviet steel, 39 per cent of metal goods, and 32 per cent of coal.

Its capital, Kiev (or Kyïv) is the oldest Slav city in the Soviet Union, and archaeologists have traced its origins back to the sixth century. It is still an important and thriving city today, with a population of about a million and a half, but it saw its heyday between 865 and 1240, when it was the capital of the strongest and biggest empire in eastern Europe, the old Kievan "Rus" state—whilst Moscow was little more than a village. At this time, it had a connection with the English royal family, for the daughter of King Harold (the one who was killed at the Battle of Hastings) was in Kiev, and married to the Emperor.

In 1709, after the battle of Poltava, Ukraine was annexed to the Muscovite Dukedom, and from 1720 onwards its historical name of "Rus" was taken over by the czars, changed to "Russia" and then applied to the whole of their empire.

Ukraine regained its independence in 1918 under the Treaty of Brest Litovsk, but this independence was to last only four years. In flagrant breach of the Treaty, the Russian Red Army conquered Ukraine and incorporated it into the Soviet Union in 1922.

Although I did not meet any whilst I was there, Ukraine is, of course, the home of the Cossacks—who live in the east of the country, far from Kiev. But the Cossack tradition lives on, especially in the Cossack dances. Indeed, although officially part of the Union of Soviet Socialist Republics, the Ukranians have managed to retain their own identity, and they are clearly anti-Russian. An example of the way in which the Ukranians feel themselves to be very much a nation in their own right was the furious reaction to a speech made by Mr. Harold Macmillan in Kiev, when he rather foolishly spoke as if he was still in Russia.

Today the Ukranian language lives on, and is still widely spoken, in spite of the fact that the official language is Russian, for most Ukranians are bilingual. But many Ukranians have left their homeland and have settled abroad. The biggest group of expatriate Ukranians are now living in Canada—the emigration of Ukranians to Canada started at the beginning of this century. Others are now in Britain, and most of these latter emigrés arrived during the last war.

Perhaps the dilemma of the Ukranians can be summed up best by quoting a few lines from the celebrated Ukranian poet, Taras Shevchenko:

> "There is no other Ukraina,
> No second Dnipro in the world,
> Yet you strike out for foreign regions,
> To seek, indeed the blessed good,
> The holy good, and freedom, freedom,
> Fraternal brotherhood. . . ."

*　　*　　*

I flew from London direct to Moscow; it was the first time I had ventured into a truly Communist country.

At the airport we were met by our interpreter, not a

31

jack-booted, beetle-browed ape, but a woman who bore the same name as Stalin's daughter—Svetlana.

But there was nothing glamorous or seductive about her. She was cold, incommunicative, and almost frighteningly masculine. She wasn't in uniform, but she might well have passed for an off-duty sergeant-major. As she escorted two colleagues and myself to the hotel I felt already that we were under close arrest.

The hotel, one of the many set aside for foreign visitors, was comfortable enough. But there was one curious and —for me at least—important omission in the furnishing. There was a bath but no plug. I checked with my colleagues; they had no plugs either.

At dinner that evening, I raised the matter with "Comrade" Svetlana. With a smile as grim as the Kremlin walls, she said seriously, "It is not usual to supply bath plugs in a hotel." Then she added, with solemn finality, "Perhaps the manufacturer of bath plugs has not been included in the present Five Year Plan."

* * *

Next day, before leaving on the train, Svetlana took us to what is known as "a friendship shop".

These shops are stocked with goods which can normally be bought only in Western countries. They are for visitors only, and only "hard" currencies are acceptable. It is pointless for Soviet citizens even to venture through the door.

I pointed out as gently as possible that if we had a shop in Britain where only foreigners could buy goods, we'd have a revolution on our hands. But I don't think she grasped the point.

Then she took us along to see Lenin's tomb—a "must" for foreigners. I asked her if Stalin's body had been placed in the sacred precincts, but she just stared back as if she didn't understand.

Finally we were escorted to the Moscow-Kiev overnight express. I noticed that there were four bunks in the carriage. Apprehensive now, and not a little dismayed, I asked her where she would be sleeping.

32

Brusquely she replied, "As there are only three of you I shall sleep in one of those bunks."

All my provincial Presbyterian inhibitions whirled in my mind and I protested that, in our country, it was not the thing for a lady to share sleeping quarters with men.

That brought a rare smile. She said scornfully, "Oh, that's a ridiculous old-fashioned idea—so bourgeois, so capitalistic." And before our bulging eyes she stripped off to her bra and panties, and slid into one of the bottom bunks.

Then, like a character in an early Hollywood comedy, she said coyly, "Well, if you three really feel embarrassed, I'll turn my face to the wall while you undress."

In the morning the woman car attendant appeared with hot water, so that we could make our own tea. The water was heated on a coke fire at the end of the corridor, the acrid fumes from which kept us coughing and spluttering all night.

There were no washing facilities, so we sat on our beds and made the most of our amateurish home brew.

None of us said a word. But I know that I had decided that if this was typical of what was in store, we weren't going to have a very happy time.

* * *

At Kiev, a mini-bus was waiting to take us north to Chernigov, a town of over 90,000 people on the banks of the Desna river. The entire countryside was flat as far as the eye could see. When we stopped to answer the call of nature, we observed that the ground was rich and black; a country with tremendous potential for foodstuffs and raw materials. But it hasn't been developed, and it is my view that Ukraine could never be fully developed except under a system of free enterprise.

At Chernigov, we were given quarters on the end of a workers' block of flats—No. 14a Karl Marx Street.

We discovered later that our accommodation had been smartened up for our benefit; the workers' flats were grim and bare, with only communal lavatories—where long queues formed, especially after working hours.

We had self-contained apartments, and again the first thing I noticed was that there were no plugs in the baths. Svetlana laughed this time—I felt she was weakening, like Greta Garbo in the film of *Ninotchka*—and said, "Ah, yes, it is still the Five Year Plan."

One evening, my colleagues were twiddling with the knobs on a short-wave radio to try to get some British news. Suddenly, loud and clear, they heard a conversation. There could be no doubt about it—the voices belonged to a German couple in a flat above.

It was immediately obvious that the Germans' apartment was being bugged, and that the radio had picked it up on the same frequency.

One of the lads nipped upstairs, and pushed a note at the surprised couple, telling them that a microphone was hidden somewhere in their bedroom. By trial and error, it was discovered that the best reception was obtained from talk near the bed.

My colleagues dismantled the bed completely, but with no result. Then, just as they had almost been persuaded that they were imagining the whole thing, they scratched at a small knot in the wooden bedhead, and out popped a tiny, but powerful microphone.

By this time the news had spread, and intensive searches were started. In one room it was discovered that a curtain-rod served as antenna for a piece of transmission equipment, and a fine wire was concealed in the hem of the curtains. In another flat, a microphone was found under a wardrobe. It was never fully established just how many "bugs" had been planted because the search was interrupted by the arrival of security police, headed by a plump, out-of-breath political commissar.

Caught red-handed, the finds had to be surrendered on the spot. But the police were furious that one piece of gear —which they claimed was valuable—couldn't be found. It transpired that one of the lads had, as a protest, hidden it. So they were confined to quarters until the missing piece was recovered.

For a time the whole thing seemed rather a joke. But after three days of being treated like erring schoolchildren it was decided to leave the missing piece in a conspicuous place so that it would be found.

This was duly done and, I suppose in the interests of friendship and commerce—or have I got that in the reverse order?—no further mention was made of the incident, and work was continued as if nothing had happened.

But it seemed pretty certain that the ordinary citizen in Ukraine had no suspicion that such things were going on.

Back home in the United Kingdom, people refer carelessly to the Union of Soviet Socialist Republics as Russia. But I soon found out that this was not acceptable in the Ukraine. In the first factory I visited I referred to being in "Russia". The men looked at one another unbelievingly and said, "You are not in Russia. You are in Ukraine. And Ukrainians must not be mistaken for Russians. We are a separate republic." I soon realized that the Ukrainians are very nationally minded, and I took good care not to repeat my gaffe.

The Ukrainians are extremely hospitable and we were often invited into their homes, although this practice is usually frowned on by the authorities in Communist countries.

A number of evenings were spent with a group of neighbors, sitting around the fire listening to a fiddler playing Ukranian folk music. And we would all sing the choruses. It reminded me forcibly of Ireland and holidays I had spent in the Western Isles of Scotland, where the people held *célidhs*.

Of all the countries I have visited, I think I'd rate the Ukrainians as being the people who are most proud of their origins and nationality. For them, Soviet Russia is very much an overlord. Their country is flooded with Soviet troops who mount guard at bridges, railway stations, and even at factory gates. The automatic rifle is their favorite weapon.

One interesting feature I noticed was that there is positively no fraternization. I don't know what orders the military had but the local folk shunned them as untouchables.

For a Ukranian to invite a Russian soldier into his house was unthinkable.

In the evenings, the dining-rooms and bars of the best hotels were full of Soviet Army officers; not a pleasing sight in their drab grey uniforms and jack-boots.

I recall an incident related by a colleague who arrived from Britain, to find that there was no accommodation in our apartments. He was put up at one of the town's hotels.

On his first evening he opened the French windows, and stepped on to the patio for a breath of summer air. Suddenly there was a click and, only a few yards away, a young woman walked on to her veranda. She was one of the most beautiful girls he had ever seen. Then, against the background of the setting sun, she slowly took off all her clothes, and stood there—stark naked.

My friend was so bewildered that he returned to his room and closed the windows—at least, so he assured me.

He knew that this was a deliberate set-up, for he had a responsible post, with access to valuable information on the latest designs of machinery for synthetic fibre plants. And I must put on record that this kind of compromising trick is much more common than is supposed. Indeed, the Number One card in Soviet Intelligence is a seductive woman.

Anyway, back in bed, his telephone rang. But when he lifted the receiver, all he could hear was a confused conversation in some unknown language. When he replaced the receiver, it immediately rang again. And again the gibberish talk. This happened several times and it became clear that he wasn't going to get much sleep that night. So he went downstairs in search of a receptionist or porter.

The hotel appeared to be deserted. Exasperated, he gave up, and went back to his bedroom.

There, at the foot of the bed, was the "veranda lady"— this time clad in a flimsy nightie. But the last thing in her mind would appear to be love-making. For she was methodically going through the contents of his briefcase.

Before he could question her, she threw the papers to the floor and bolted along the corridor.

When he reported this to the interpreter next morning,

he received the bland reply, "Oh, don't make an issue of a trivial act. She probably had too much vodka, and didn't know what she was doing. Forget about it."

A few weeks later, however, on a similar hot summer night, I couldn't sleep, and went out to the patio. The street lights had long since been extinguished and it was dark.

I could see some movement in the shadows below and, as my eyes grew accustomed to the gloom, I saw a man and a woman. He lifted her up till she was on his shoulders and she climbed through a ground-floor window.

Oddly, I didn't think of burglars. I assumed that they were just a courting couple who had been locked out of the building. I had heard that one of our colleagues was walking out with a Russian girl—*not* a Ukrainian, but a Russian who had moved into the district and was employed as a technician in our factory.

I thought little more about this until, some nights later, just dropping off to sleep, I heard crying and screaming; obviously a woman, and in great pain.

I seized a dressing gown and ran outside, to be joined by about half the residents, all in night attire. There, lying on the footpath, was the young lady who had been hoisted through the window. Her leg was broken.

Her companion of a few nights before was lending a hand to get her carried inside. It was only then that I noticed something that absolutely stunned me—he was in police uniform. Did this mean that one of my own colleagues was being subverted by a Communist? Had he fallen into the same trap as many others who have gone to the Soviet Union on business?

I have thought a lot about those incidents and I am firmly convinced that there must be many businessmen in the West who have had undue pressure put on them by Soviet Intelligence. I am not suggesting that they are at Government level, but I am nevertheless sure that they are able to provide useful economic information.

At this stage it would be appropriate to refer to the book *Sailor in a Russian Frame*[1] by Commander Anthony

---

[1] Johnson Publications Ltd.

Courtney, who describes the way in which the Russians tried to frame him, and presents the view that the government should declare an amnesty to all in similar situations.

* * *

I am very much a lone wolf by disposition. On many evenings I'd leave the apartment, and stroll for about half a mile into the main square, and have a meal in the nearest hotel. Usually fish and vegetables, because meat is very scarce in that area. Indeed, it is well known in London that when visitors from the Soviet Union arrive, they should be offered roast beef or steaks.

After dinner I would sit outside at a pavement table with a final drink. Almost without realizing it, I became aware of a "regular"—an old man who passed by and always nodded and smiled.

One night I was there with a cup of black coffee and a reasonably drinkable brandy in front of me; he came over, bowed respectfully and gestured, obviously asking if he might sit down.

To my amazement, he spoke English. He chatted amicably and asked me what I was doing there; he looked me firmly in the eye and said, "Do you believe? Are you a church member? Or—forgive me for asking—are you by any chance an atheist?"

I sensed by the tone of his voice, the emphasis put on the words, and the almost hypnotic stare of his eyes that this was a most important question.

I looked at him levelly.

"Yes," I replied, "I am a member of the Christian Church—a practicing member."

He looked at me with relief and, indeed, with approval.

Then he said, "Tomorrow night I should like you to come to my home. It would be dangerous to attract attention so I shall not meet you here, but opposite the park."

My curiosity was really aroused. After dinner next evening I was strolling past the park when I heard someone calling me.

It was my friend of the night before.

38

When we arrived at his house we were greeted by a large group of relatives. His wife was an aged, wrinkled, parchment-faced woman. I could see that her days in this world were certainly numbered.

He motioned me to sit down on a wooden chair. Nobody spoke. They all looked at me—friendly, but tentatively.

The old man went upstairs with his son and I could hear the sound of furniture being moved and scraping across the floor.

Within minutes he reappeared, carrying a parcel.

With dignity he carried it across the room—not held close to him, but with arms outstretched. The thought flashed through my mind that he looked like an archbishop bearing a sacred relic.

Slowly, with what seemed unnecessarily elaborate care, he undid the outer coverings of faded newspapers, and laid the contents on the scrubbed deal table.

One frequently uses the phrase "I couldn't believe me eyes". But that describes exactly my reaction in that revealing moment.

There, spread out in the soft glow of the oil lamps were ancient religious paintings in embossed frames, together with a richly engraved cross.

They were obviously icons used in worship. I examined them with care. I had never seen such superb craftsmanship.

And I told the old man as much. His face glowed with pride, and he said, "I am glad. These are family icons. As you can see, they go back many, many years."

He hesitated, turned round to look enquiringly at the family. They nodded.

He lowered his voice, and added, "And these are from the cathedral at Kiev. We saved them before the cathedral was sacked by the Communists."

He paused, and looked hard at me. Then, in a persuasive tone, he said, "Take them. Please take them," and he pushed them towards me.

I had been accustomed to foreigners handing me little

39

gifts as souvenirs to take home, but nothing on this lavish scale.

I told him that I couldn't possibly accept; it was out of the question.

The old man said softly, but with great solemnity and dignity, "Take them. Take them—to our countrymen in the world outside—the world that is still free. What is the good of having them here when we cannot display them publicly, when they cannot be treated with the respect and reverence they deserve."

I was in a quandary. I was so afraid to get involved in a controversy, or say anything of which he might disapprove. At the same time, I was reluctant to offend the susceptibilities of an old man who clearly had so little time left.

Suddenly, the problem was solved for me. His wife must have sensed my embarrassment. She rose from her chair, came slowly across the room, and took both my hands in her own wrinkled ones. She looked up at me imploringly, and the tears welled up in her rheumy eyes. That did it. I hadn't then the heart to refuse.

I parcelled the icons up, carefully and gently. Then I shook hands all round, and went back to my quarters.

The question now was—what to do with the icons? How was I to transport them safely to the free world?

*   *   *

I was due to return home on leave in a few weeks' time, and I had scrounged a tea chest, because I had volunteered to take back some surplus pieces of equipment to my company in Britain, together with a few personal belongings.

So I wrapped the icons carefully inside woollen cardigans and pajamas, and packed them into the tea chest. I then put a piece of plywood over them. At first glance it would look like the bottom of the chest.

I was taking a tremendous risk, as the Soviet authorities scrupulously examined every item taken out of the country. The drill to get stuff through was to ask an interpreter to vouch for your belongings, and sign a clearance form. The suitcase or box would then be sealed, and go straight through Customs.

I had what I hoped was a shrewd idea. I plumped for my favorite interpreter, a woman.

She was small, frigid, always complaining about her health—and neurotic about cleanliness. She went through the stuff on top of the tea chest, and checked it against my list. Then she reached the pieces of equipment, thick with dirty oil. I had anticipated exactly how she would react. She drew back her hands in disgust, and said, "Oh, let us not go any further. . . . They look as if they'd come out of a sewer."

The box was sealed in my presence, and she signed the clearance chit—having first cleansed her beautifully manicured hands with disinfectant. I could almost hear her assuring her comrades later that, of course, the Irish lived like pigs.

*   *   *

I recall one evening walking through the park with this interpreter when we saw an enormous stone plinth. Obviously, it had at one time borne a statue.

She said, "That was a statue of Stalin. But when we discovered that he was not following the correct policy, we knocked it down. We got our sledgehammers out for the job."

I looked at this frail little woman and said, jokingly, "Did you have a go with a sledge-hammer?" She replied with burning seriousness, "Certainly. I helped, in my fashion, to smash the statue into little pieces—as small as possible." Then she added, with a sigh of self-pity, "But I'm afraid I found the hammer too heavy."

I suggested that they had, perhaps, been a little premature.

Supposing, overnight, they discovered that Stalin was right after all? What then? They might have to go to all the trouble and expense of erecting new statues.

"For more than half a century, two hundred million people were convinced that Stalin was correct in every respect. Suddenly you turned against him, and against his memory."

She looked astonished and said, "But how were we to know? We had not been informed. But as soon as we did, we took immediate action—to remove all traces."

Wryly I said, "Stalin must have been a very clever man to fool you all for fifty years. I still think it would have been wiser to put Stalin's statues in storage."

I thought then—and my colleagues agreed—that this must surely have been the most successful exercise in mass brain-conditioning that the world has seen.

But how wrong we were. Little did I guess then that, only a few weeks after my return to Britain, I was destined for a posting to Red China, where I would witness the so-called Cultural Revolution.

*　　*　　*

Eventually the time arrived for me to leave Ukraine. I caught the overnight express from Kiev to Moscow.

The train was still without a restaurant, but there was a bar of sorts—for tea and soft drinks. I was standing there, making the most of a warm lemonade in a grubby plastic mug when the attendant banged on the counter with a spoon and made an announcement. He put tins of "instant coffee" up for sale.

Miraculously, the word spread along the train. Scores of shouting, pushing travellers—Russians and Ukrainians—crammed into the buffet car. Within seconds, the tins of instant coffee had disappeared.

For me the other point of interest on that journey was the presence of Arab students from Kiev University returning to the Middle East. They had wads of useless Soviet currency, and they were trying to exchange it for hard currency—at seven times the official rate.

One can usually change Soviet roubles into hard currency equalling the amount that has been brought into the country. When I heard those students offering *seven* times the official rate, I had some indication of the true value of the Russian rouble.

Back in Britain, I asked some of my Ukrainian friends in London about the smuggled icons. They were most impressed. I asked, perhaps naively, what they were worth. I meant in money. One of them looked at me with awe, and said, "If you had been caught with these, George, you'd have got twenty years' hard labor in Siberia."

That really made my heart jump. Anyway I had the icons examined by Ukrainian scholars in Britain and it was established that they came from one of the cathedrals in Kiev. They were genuine Ukrainian icons. Most of them were *ex-voto* offerings from families in Kiev to the Cathedral (now, alas, an anti-religious museum), where they had been kept in the crypt. One of the icons contains a handwritten dedication in the Ukrainian language from a father to his son. The cross, on the other hand, is even older than the icons and is undoubtedly of liturgical origin.

These treasures had been saved from the advancing Communists by the Christian underground, and had remained hidden for almost half a century until I was destined to meet—accidentally—the Christian underground of Ukraine. I felt proud then, and am still proud today, that I became the instrument of bringing back those precious and priceless objects of a people striving for religious and political freedom.

In conclusion, let me repeat that I found the Ukrainians nationally minded. They are a closely-knit people and are firmly anti-Communist. I personally am confident that the day is not far distant when they will overthrow the Soviet Army of Occupation, and once again regain their freedom.

Although it was over a hundred years ago, actually in 1845, when the Ukrainian poet Taras Shevchenko wrote these lines, I feel that his words are still relevant today:

"Find your wits! Be human beings,
For evil is impending,
Very soon the shackled people
Will their chains be rending;
Judgment will come, and then shall speak
The mountains and the Dnipro,

And in a hundred rivers, blood
Will flow to the blue ocean."

Because I have brought back their icons to the Western world, I feel that I have also brought the proof of a people striving for freedom. May I say to the Ukrainians that I am honored.

CHAPTER IV

Assignment: China

Two weeks before Christmas 1966 I was on my way from London to Red China, and I well recall the excitement I felt at the prospect of seeing this vast, strange land.

The first snag occurred when I had to wait in Peking for five days. I was to learn that in China one doesn't just walk across an airport runway to board another aircraft. To catch a connecting flight one may well be forced to sit around for a week or more—the Chinese won't think of putting a machine into the air if the weather is even slightly unfavorable.

I was accompanied on the outward flight from London by an Englishman from Bolton, Lancashire, and it was while we were waiting in the Hsin-Chiao Hotel, Peking, that I got my first insight into the peculiar way things happen in Red China.

For example, we met some businessmen who had been marooned in the hotel, not for weeks, but for months— just waiting for appointments to sell their products. The firms who deal with China know now what to expect and it follows that if a big company wants to sell machinery or plant to China, they won't waste time and money sending a high-powered executive to spend months cooling his heels in some hotel lobby. They send small fry instead, but, as camouflage, adorn him with a high-flown title— such as Senior Sales Administrator. Then he will sit there while the months go by, until such time as the Chinese decide to enter into serious negotiations. They will then allow him to get in touch with senior colleagues in Britain, and visas will be granted for these latter to fly out to clinch the deal.

A businessman will sometimes leave the hotel for a stroll in the park. The minute he returns, an interpreter will rush up, and say, apologetically, "Mr. Jones, where have you been? We've been looking for you everywhere. If only we'd known, we could have fitted in an interview this afternoon, and started the preliminary discussions."

So everyone just resigned themselves to hanging around the top floor of the Hsin-Chiao Hotel, becoming expert at playing billiards. It was agreed that the British and the Japanese have the most patience; they are prepared to dig themselves in for months on end, whereas the Spanish and Italians, in true Latin fashion, tend to get a little bit excited, and blow their tops. They don't seem to have adapted themselves to playing this long, drawn-out cat-and-mouse game.

I remember a businessman coming in one evening beaming like a Cheshire cat. He had gone along to make a most flattering speech, praising Mao for his intelligence, and stressing that he was the true leader of the Chinese people, irrespective of the claims of any imposter.

We asked him what was so remarkable about this, for it was generally understood that they were suckers for flattery. We had already seen giant notices posted everywhere proclaiming that they were the great Chinese race, and most businessmen, trying hard to keep a straight face, introduced the most lavish flattery in their speeches.

It transpired that, a few months before, our friend had been to Free China—he had two passports—and made a magnificent speech, praising Generalissimo Chiang Kai-Shek. When he returned, all he had to do was keep this speech intact, and substitute Mao for every reference to Chiang.

I mention this because it is typical of the many amusing little tricks businessmen played, partly to relieve the tedium of waiting for so long.

One day, whilst still waiting in Peking, our interpreter,

Mr. Gin, offered to take my colleagues and myself on a sight-seeing trip. We visited a new building called The Great Hall. The Chinese word for "great" is *"da"*; and very few slogans are written in which *"da"* doesn't appear. On the side of the hall was a massive portrait of their leader, Mao. Suddenly I noticed a marked similarity in Mao's dress to the kind of uniform worn by West Africa's Nkrumah—the same high-buttoned collar. I said to the interpreter, "Isn't that so like the Great Helmsman?" which was how Nkrumah liked to be styled. Affably, Mr. Gin agreed that the picture was indeed a splendid likeness of the Great Helmsman; and I realized that, coincidentally, Mao had adopted this title for himself.

I recalled that Nkrumah had called himself the Great Teacher and the Father of the Nation. So, hoping I wasn't stretching the sarcasm too much, I assured Mr. Gin that Chairman Mao was the Great Teacher and the Father of the Chinese Nation. He beamed, clapped me on the shoulder, and said, "Ah, I see that you have heard these titles before."

For my final joke, as it were, I added, "Mao is the world's greatest statesman and the leader of all the Asian people."

Mr. Gin solemnly replied, *"No.* He is not. Mao is the greatest genius of all time, and the leader of *all* the people in the world."

When I looked at him I could see that Mr Gin seriously believed this. I hadn't the heart—or the courage—to tell him how many so-called Socialist heads of State have given themselves those grand titles.

* * *

On my fourth day in Peking I went round to the British Mission to pay my respects to the diplomats; something one usually does in underdeveloped countries. It is always a wise move in Communist countries, too, where foreigners can vanish without trace. I invited Mr. Gin to come with me, but he appeared to be terrified at the very thought.

Chairman Mao doesn't encourage any kind of illicit relations with foreign governments.

The Mission building in Peking is in the centre of a big residential area for diplomats. The living quarters for British diplomats are only about fifty yards from the main building, I mention this here because it has some bearing on what happened a year later when—on 22 August, 1967 —the Red Guards sacked the Mission.

On another occasion during my stay in Peking Mr. Gin, our eternal watchdog, decided that my colleague and I should visit the Peking War Museum.

To be honest, I wasn't interested in the least, for although I was subsequently to be accused of stealing important military intelligence, the truth is that I have never received any kind of military training. I hadn't the remotest idea how to put a bullet into a gun—let alone fire it with any degree of accuracy.

But out of courtesy I agreed with Mr. Gin's suggestion, and the three of us spent the afternoon inspecting the remains of shot-down aircraft—all of them, incidentally, obsolete models.

There were also captured arms and ammunition from the pre-Communist era. The odd thing was that our interpreter took obvious delight in pointing to a rusting, out-of-date Vickers machine gun.

Looking at me, he announced with an almost triumphant sneer: "Vickers-Zimmer", the name of my employers.

I tried to maintain a poker-straight face, and flashed a smile which I hoped was non-committal. Inwardly, I was alarmed that the name of Vickers was not unknown to the Communists in the military sense. I had hoped that they would think that our company was engaged only in the chemical and synthetic fibres field.

To my astonishment Mr. Gin then quoted one of the "Thoughts" of Chairman Mao which, I was later to realize, the masses are compelled—and I mean compelled—to learn off by heart and chant in unison.

The gist of this so-called "Thought" proclaimed that imperialist capitalist groups depended on aggression for their profits. He ended by emphasizing the word "Vickers".

I recall now that, on our silent journey by taxi back to the Hsin-Chiao Hotel, I was filled with apprehension and a strong, though vague, foreboding.

Later that evening, I had the uneasy feeling, that, because of the visit to the war museum and the sinister jibe at Vickers, we were perhaps starting this journey into the great unknown on the wrong foot.

Little did I realize that so many years would pass, during which I would suffer hardship and even torture by the secret police, before I would eventually escape from the Communist cobweb back into freedom and civilization.

CHAPTER V

Lanchow: The Atomic City

At last I received clearance to leave Peking, and on the afternoon of 19 December, 1966, I was in a small Russian-built aircraft somewhere over Central China, about 40 minutes' flight from my final destination—the old walled city of Lanchow. On the banks of the Yellow River, Lanchow is the ancient capital of the mountainous province of Kansu, which is said to be the wildest region in China.

But I was not allowed to see Lanchow and its surrounds from the air. Thirty minutes before landing, all curtains were drawn, and passengers were instructed not to look out. It transpired that somewhere beneath us was one of China's main atomic stations.

At the airport I was met by a reception committee. All were dressed in dark blue uniforms, with no badges of rank. They bowed and smiled. Around us were hundreds of chattering men and women, a few Red Guards, and even a dance troupe complete with gongs and cymbals.

The group put on a special performance for myself and another engineer from Britain who was joining the firm's project in Lanchow. The noise was terrific, but their faces were happy and smiling as they gathered to observe the strange "long noses"—the name by which all Europeans are known.

Above the din, the interpreter shouted. "This is to welcome you to China, and to propagate the works of Chairman Mao."

The 30-minute drive from the airport was rather dreary, along a dusty road bordered by unkempt grass verges. Occasionally I saw a wayside stall with fruit for sale. The only vehicles on the road were huge grey lorries which, like my taxi, were Russian-built.

Even then, I didn't see Lanchow, because the Friendship Hotel, where all foreign visitors are housed, is three miles from the city's main gates.

In the well of the hotel entrance, below the staircase stood a large bust of Mao Tse-tung, overlaid in gold leaf and mounted on an 8ft-tall pedestal.

My room was drab, dusty, and could hardly be called comfortable. The bed springs were of stout wire mesh; the hard mattress, packed with some kind of animal hair, was only about two inches thick.

The room had central heating; unfortunately, the radiators seldom worked. I had a private bathroom, but there was seldom hot water in the tap.

The biggest hazard was the cockroaches. Like the portraits of Chairman Mao, they were everywhere—and larger than life. In China, one seldom sees a dog or a cat, or even a house-fly, but cockroaches appear to lead a charmed existence.

Dinner at the hotel that night was far from the expected banquet of oriental splendor. It consisted of roast pork, fried rice, and vegetables, followed by steamed currant pudding and some sort of gooey custard. This was washed down with two bottles of Chinese beer—which I found palatable—and tea. I never had coffee during the whole of the time I was there. Contrary to what one might expect, tea is for the ordinary Chinese worker an unheard-of luxury, and the normal drink is hot water.

So far as I could judge, the Chinese had no luxuries. A shop attached to the hotel sold fruit, tomatoes, and soap. One could also buy unsweetened black chocolate and simple boiled sweets. But there was nothing extravagant.

Once I saw soap powder. Not in colorful packets, but

in 2oz portions in plain brown envelopes. They were strictly rationed to 6oz for each person.

After dinner that evening, the interpreter—our ubiquitous Mr. Gin—briefed me on what I could and could
not do in Lanchow. It took two hours, I cannot now recall
everything he said, but the main points were:

'I must not, in any circumstances, hold the hand of a
Chinese girl, or be "familiar" with her. Even a friendly
smile to a waitress, he pointed out, might be mis-
construed.

'I must not take photographs of anything or anybody
without obtaining permission. I was not to enter Chinese
homes, and I was not to leave the Friendship Hotel
without an interpreter.

'There was no place outside the hotel where Europeans could eat. I could go shopping only on Saturday
afternoons. Finally, the hotel doors would be locked
each night at 10 sharp.'

* * *

I was astonished by this list of rules; but I recall now
that at the time I didn't resent them.

Then Mr. Gin treated me to a long explanation of the
idea behind the Cultural Revolution, adding gratuitously
that they did not approve of "yellow music"—meaning
jazz and pop.

I quipped feebly, "You certainly lay on a humdinger of
a time for your visitors." Mr. Gin didn't appreciate the
joke. None of them ever do.

At this point, I did not realize that I had arrived in
China as the Cultural Revolution was about to reach its
peak of barbarism. And little did I guess that I was to be
one of its hapless victims.

The first few days passed pleasantly enough. Work on
the site at the textile factory kept me occupied. In the
evenings, I would join one or two of the five British people,
working on various projects, to stroll along the banks of

the Yellow River, or into the city, a grey-brown place of shabby antiquity.

Most of the men and women wore blue or brown trouser suits of thin cotton, quilted on top for the fierce winters.

Always the Red Guards were on parade. I never once went for a walk without seeing at least two or three groups of a dozen or more.

Sometimes, there were hundreds of them with whistles and drums and gongs, always the distinguishing six-inch wide red band on their arms. In those days, they seemed harmless enough.

Like all Chinese, they would stop to stare curiously whenever a European appeared. They would touch the material of your suit, perhaps touch your face or hand. One actually pulled up my trousers to look at my legs. But it was all nothing more than friendly curiosity.

At the entrance to the vegetable market one afternoon I saw a row of a dozen beggars, squatting on their haunches and holding out cups.

I said to Mr. Gin, "I thought there were no beggars in the new China."

With a completely straight face, he replied, "That is true. There are no beggars in the new China."

"But," I said, "what then are those men doing?"

Calmly, he answered, "Begging."

"Then," I pursued, with dogged logic, "If they are begging, they must be beggars."

Mr. Gin stared at me, without changing his expression. "Yes," he said slowly, "they are beggars. But you must understand that they are not doing it *officially*. There are no beggars in the new China."

*   *   *

As we had arrived in Lanchow only a few days before Christmas, I decided to ask the Chinese if they could arrange something special for Christmas Day dinner. I think the irony of the situation appealed to my Irish sense of humor—sitting down to celebrate the Christmas fes-

51

tival in this land of Communism and unbelief; and, of all places, in Lanchow, the secret atomic city in the very heart —or should I say the entrails?—of Red China.

They indicated that they had at least heard of our Christian "holiday". I didn't expect any of the gourmets' delights from the Western world, and we didn't even aspire to turkey and plum pudding, far less peacocks' tongues in aspic. All of us European residents realized by this time that even ordinary beef was impossible to get. Humbly, I suggested that we'd be happy to settle for pork. Perhaps roast piglet—maybe even with an apple in its mouth for decoration?—anything, indeed, to alleviate the dreary atmosphere.

Imagine our delight that Christmas evening to find not one but two piglets on the table. They looked brown and succulent, *and* each had an apple in its mouth.

Could this be true? Surely it couldn't be happening in Communist China, after all the tales we'd heard of such squalor and poverty. At that moment, I couldn't decide if London's Savoy or New York's Waldorf Astoria could have produced a comparable *chef d'oeuvre*.

That Christmas Night meal was memorable for me in more than one sense. Feeling slightly contrite because of my previous suspicions and churlishness, I took the interpreter aside to thank him.

"Oh, it was no trouble at all," he said blandly. "We wouldn't have eaten the piglets, anyway. You see, *they died at birth.*"

I felt my stomach heave, and made smartly for the lavatory, where I disposed of my Christmas dinner.

*   *   *

One day, walking along the Yellow River with the interpreter a procession arrived, with everyone carrying little objects. Suddenly they threw them into the stream.

The interpreter explained that those were religious figures—idols and statuettes associated with various religious beliefs. Some threw crucifixes, Bibles, effigies of "The

52

Laughing Buddha", all of which were at one time held in esteem and treasured.

I suggested that Communist countries had firmly emphasized that they believed in religious freedom—religion was perhaps not openly encouraged, but it was not forbidden. What, then, was happening now?

He replied that this was a new order from the local military commander and political commissars that the area should be "purified from religious and superstitious practices". All evidence associated with organized religion, however trivial, was to be destroyed.

I think it's worth mentioning that this wasn't the first time I had witnessed anti-religious feeling. Only a few monhs earlier, in Ukraine, I had seen the doors of churches nailed up with wooden battens, and windows blacked out.

The Chinese, however, appeared to be more disciplined than the Russians. Although on the one hand Chairman Mao has set himself up as a god, a super-being, he has instructed the masses of the Chinese people through one of his "Thoughts" that they should destroy individualism.

This is an attempt to condition them towards a state of —let me invent my own word—ROBOTISATION.

On the other hand, the Chinese also have what is known as "points of liberalism"—though ironically enough, the word "liberalism" has never in my view been so abused as it is today in Communist China.

The masses are told to watch each other, and listen for any hint of "reactionary remarks". Anything that appears, however slightly, to be critical of Mao or the Communist system is classified as "reactionary".

Anyone who makes a reactionary remark is liable to punishment. But—and this is important—it is also an offense to *hear* a reactionary remark and just take it lightly; in other words, forget about it. It must be reported.

After some research, I have been able to pinpoint the teaching exactly. It is officially called "The Sixth Point of Liberalism".

It goes like this:

"To hear incorrect views without rebutting them . . .

and even to hear counter-revolutionary remarks without reporting them . . . and, instead, to receive them calmly as if nothing had happened."

This is part of an instruction given by Mao on 7 September, 1937. And it is used today to help keep the people of Communist China in bondage.

In accord with this edict, fathers must report their sons, and children their parents. The system pacticed under this Sixth Point of Liberalism is closely akin to the vicious family-destroying policy propagated by Hitler in Nazi Germany.

Is it any wonder then that there is so little spoken opposition to the Mao régime in Communist China?

Even if one were courageous enough to speak out, everyone listening would immediately be in peril of their lives. It would take a bold man indeed to challenge the Sixth Point of Liberalism.

The Seventh Point of Liberalism is equally sinister. This is practiced by Communist agitators engaged in industrial and economic sabotage in Western countries.

Mao also declared on 7 September, 1937:

"To be among the masses, and fail to conduct propaganda, speak at meetings, or conduct investigations and enquiries."

To fail under the direct, watchful eye of the secret police to adhere rigidly to those two points, the Sixth and Seventh, can only end with the offender being incarcerated in a labor camp.

A labor camp is now known as a "remolding center"; and brainwashing as "becoming enlightened".

Everywhere I went I could see signs of this tremendous and terrible pressure; people appeared to walk under a permanent cloud of fear.

I remember my interpreter saying to me, rather wistfully, I thought, that some day he would like to visit his young wife who was teaching English in Wuhan University. As things stood, he wouldn't be able to see her for at least five years.

In my ignorance I failed to see what the problem was. I said, rather airily, "What are you waiting for, man? Pack up here, and go and get a job where your wife is!" Even in the so-called bad old days, in Britain, I told him, no one had been forcibly held in their place of employment; they had been free to leave.

Sadly, I discovered that the Marxists in China have chained themselves; they are far from being free to change their jobs and go somewhere else, even when it is to rejoin their lawful wives. It is impressed on them that they are the property of the State; the political commissars will decide where they go—and when. I came to the conclusion that Communist China must be the world's largest prison. Indeed, one of the things that struck me forcibly about Red China was the disintegration of family life as we in the West know it.

Labor resources are considered to be completely mobile and it happens time and time again that one or other of the marriage partners is sent to work in some remote province, hundreds of miles away from the family home. If there are young children, the normal practice is to put them in nursery schools, where they are suitably indoctrinated with Chinese Communist ideology.

I then heard that other interpreters were under what was called "criticism" because they had expressed a desire to marry when they were considered to be too young. The authorities decreed that to think about marrying under thirty was "much too young", even irresponsible.

Others were also under "criticism" for having families that were considered too large.

It is difficult, if not impossible, for people reared in freedom-loving countries to appreciate this kind of calculated, refined barbarism, this utter negation of the dignity of human life.

CHAPTER VI

Our First Contretemps

Towards the end of my first week in Lanchow I was taking a Sunday walk with a British colleague accompanied—as always—by Mr. Gin. About a quarter of a mile from the hotel, near the bank of the Yellow River, we saw a group of Red Guards ahead of us. They were shouting, blowing whistles, and were clearly highly excited.

One of them carried a bundle. Suddenly, he threw the bundle to the ground, and they all gathered round. Waving red books containing the Thoughts of Mao, they chanted, *"Wa, wa, wa"*. Then they walked on, still cheering.

When we walked over to the bundle, I could see that it contained the nude body of a boy, perhaps three or four years old. He was dead, and had been badly burned.

It was my first taste of the savagery which could be so suddenly unleashed. I felt physically sick.

My colleague and I looked at each other, horrified. Then I felt Mr. Gin pulling at my sleeve. He said "Come along, now. No photographs." And he took my camera.

Months later, I was to learn that this was a fairly common form of action against "enemies of the people". A wife, husband, or child would be maltreated, or killed, to intimidate the offender's family.

That evening a political commissar arrived at the hotel to warn me that I must not spread alarming rumors. I assured him that I was not spreading any rumors, and he seemed to be a little mollified. I added that I had only mentioned casually the incident we'd seen on the banks of the Yellow River. He shouted, "That's exactly what I mean."

I was soon to experience fear myself.

Two senior Chinese engineers had invited all the Europeans at the Friendship Hotel—there were about 30 of us, British and German, with one or two wives and a few children—to dinner.

The meal was much better than usual, and the wine

flowed. One of our hosts, who could speak English, made a speech explaining that the dinner was to welcome us to China.

At that time work at the site wasn't going along too well, because the Chinese workers habitually downed tools, during working hours, to read Mao's thoughts, to hold discussion groups, or just—in my opinion—because they were bone idle.

Our dinner host said, "We are well aware that some of the men are not working too assiduously, and that progress is slow. We realize that much time is spent in making speeches and holding discussions. But that is the way of the new China. We must try to be patient, and see if we can improve the pace of progress in the future."

Nothing happened till two days later.

Mr. Gin, knowing I was interested in antiques, suggested I might like to visit a curio shop in the city. It is situated in a corner of a wide open space called Anti-Revisionist Square. As we approached the shop, the square was filled with a howling mob.

Then I caught sight of my host of two nights before. He was strung up by the neck to a lamp-post, and he was dead.

I turned to Mr. Gin for explanation . . . "Why, in God's name, why?"

Solemnly, he told me, "That man has been punished for a number of crimes. He chose to take the capitalist road, and lord it over his comrades by wasting public funds on high living, and needlessly entertaining foreigners."

As he spoke, Mr. Gin studied my face, trying to gauge my reaction. His eyes never blinked.

I felt guilty; and in a way partly to blame for that unfortunate man's death. I was sure I had been brought to the scene so that my reactions could be tested.

I tried to maintain an impassive face. I managed to shrug as if I cared nothing. I said in a clear voice, "Yes, that is most interesting," and walked into the curio shop.

*   *   *

On New Year's Eve, when I had been in Lanchow for

only 13 days, one of the interpreters—there were always three on duty at the hotel—asked a group of Europeans if they would care to celebrate the occasion with firecrackers.

Thinking of the children, we accepted immediately. The interpreter explained that the firecrackers would be available at the hotel shop that afternoon. He omitted to add that we should have to pay for them.

It was a splendid, carefree evening. The crackers were let off on the flat roof of the hotel, and the children were delighted. It was probably one of the happiest moments of their stay in China.

I think now that the children's obvious pleasure—and the excellent beer—lowered our customary guard. Later that same evening, in my room—which the British called George's Inn, and the Germans' Paddy's Bar—we all found ourselves thinking well of the Chinese.

One of the Germans, Herr von Xylander, son of the late Lieutenant-General Xylander, said, "It is strange how these people can be so kind, at times. Perhaps they are not really so bad as we think."

I ought to point out that Xylander himself was later arrested, accused of being a political spy, interrogated by the secret police in Lanchow for two years, until he signed confessions, and was sentenced to ten years' imprisonment in solitary confinement. He is still in the People's Republic of China.

Anyway, I agreed with Xylander that evening. But next morning my views changed abruptly.

It was New Year's Day, 1967. Soon after daylight, Red Guards arrived at the hotel, and complained that one of our firecrackers had hit a passing cyclist in the face. His cheekbone had been fractured, and he was now in hospital.

It was believed, said the Guards, that this was "a premeditated act of provocation against the Chinese People".

It was so patently ridiculous that no one said anything for a moment; we were stunned. Then four of us asked to see the man.

The crowds outside the hospital were so thick that police

had to force a way for us. We found the "injured" man in bed, one side of his face covered with gauze and cotton wool.

His room was crowded with Red Guards. A woman who, we were told, was his wife, sat by the bed, her face completely expressionless.

Nothing more was said, and we were hustled back to the hotel. But next day, Mr. Gin told us, "News of what has happened is spreading through the city. The people are angry. They are demanding action, and you are going to be put on trial by the Red Guards."

Now, there was a curious feature of the man's injuries that was never explained. If he had been injured in the way described, and if he had in fact been cycling past the hotel in the direction stated, his wound would have been on the *other* side of his face.

* * *

Four of us, the Vickers site manager, Robert Barnes, myself, and our opposite numbers from the West German Lurgi company, suggested that we should attend the trial as representatives of the whole European group. When the Chinese agreed to this, our relief was enormous; for we had been fairly sure that they would insist on dragging in the children.

The trial lasted until nearly the end of January. It was held in one of the hotel reception rooms. The Chinese authorities said that to hold it in the city would be too dangerous for us.

The four of us were taken to the "court" several times during those weeks. The sessions would last two or three hours, and always the room was full of Red Guards—leering, shouting, and pointing at us. Again and again we were told the same thing: "You are guilty. There is no point in denying the truth. In your own interests, you should write a good confession."

Slowly, I was beginning to realize that the Chinese mentality demands that they are always right, and they must always win.

Nevertheless, we refused to confess to something of

which we were totally innocent. We were, in fact, playing for time, trying to work a way in which the women and children could be left out of this inhuman farce.

The man in charge of this so-called trial was a youngster. He looked no more than 20. He repeatedly lost his temper, and treated us to a stream of abuse . . . "Imperialist lackeys—running dogs—swine." All this hurled at us with a mad, twisted mouth that looked near to frothing.

Finally, he warned us, "Your attitude is going from bad to worse. Not only have you injured a comrade, but you are now insulting him, and his revolutionary spirit."

I looked around this kangaroo court, where we had no legal or any other representative, and met the blazing eyes in those hate-charged faces that surrounded us. We were allowed to speak only when given permission. My spirits really plummeted. I tried to close my senses to the venom and the noise, and stood there thinking about my wife and family in England.

I wondered if I would ever see them again.

Then I heard Mr. Gin translating a new charge, referring to New Year's Eve. He said, "You were celebrating an occasion based on a combination of religion and superstition. That in itself is a serious crime, and an additional act of provocation against the masses."

This outrageously ridiculous charge had the effect of snapping back some fight into me.

"Then, why," I shouted, "did you offer the fireworks to us? If it is a crime for us to celebrate, why didn't you warn us, instead of slyly encouraging us? You set this whole thing up to trap us."

I was furious. But one of the four muttered, "Steady on, George. Take it easy." I just managed to choke back my words. But, inside, I thought "You Communist bastards. You cunning, evil bastards."

Oddly, not a lot of notice was taken of my outburst. My tormentors merely pointed at me, and said:

"The condition of the injured man is getting worse, and so is your position. . . . The masses are demanding blood for blood, and they will take your blood."

Back in my room that evening, we held a conference. What could be done?

Then I had a brainwave.

At least, I thought it was a smart idea at the time, and so did everyone else.

Before I left Britain, my head office in London had been told that an enginer who had fallen ill was unable to get antibiotic treatment in Lanchow hospital. It was decided that I should bring out an emergency supply for our own people. I still had the antibiotics—unwrapped.

Pulling out my suitcase, I said, "Let's give them all those antibiotics. They are determined to show that we injured this man, but this may indicate that we are not so bad after all, that we wish to help them."

I went to Mr. Gin to explain our offer. Like all Chinese, he wouldn't give me an immediate or unqualified answer. But at my urging, he telephoned the political commissar.

Putting down the telephone, Mr. Gin said, "You have been granted permission to take the drugs to the hospital."

"Come along, then," I shouted, and we ran for a taxi.

But at the hospital, it took ten minutes to cover the 15 yards from the taxi to the door. Police and troops had to help me force a way through the crowd. They were screaming abuse at me. I was punched and pulled and pushed as I tried to get through. Hands clawed at my hair and clothes. Some of the crowd spat at me in their fury.

By the time I got inside, I was bruised, and my clothes were torn. But I still had that package of antibiotics intact, and I was feeling pretty good as Mr. Gin led the way into the injured man's ward.

A retinue of Red Guards stood by his bed. His wife was there, too, and four men in white coats whom I took to be doctors. I made to shake hands, but all four clasped their hands behind their backs.

Then complete disillusion! Perhaps I ought to have been prepared for it; but at that time I didn't even begin to understand the Chinese.

One of the doctors, in a voice loaded with loathing, addressed me as I stood there holding out the parcel—nobody had made a move to take it from me. . . .

"Are you trying to insult us? You have come here to belittle us by suggesting that we are unable to supply antibiotics."

I just stared at him in disbelief. I couldn't think of anything to say.

Turning to go, I pushed the package into the hands of the nearest doctor. He didn't hand it back. We never saw those drugs again.

Once more, I had to run the gauntlet of the crowd to reach the taxi. As I lay back in the seat, I felt dazed. I also felt very frightened.

That evening, we asked permission to telephone the office of the British *Chargé d'Affaires* in Peking. To my surprise, this request was granted. But a call to Peking, which normally took six to eight hours to get through, did not materialize this time for two days. I concluded that this was all part of the procedure to make us sweat.

When the call did come through, two or three of us took it in turn to speak to the British diplomats. Their advice was very guarded.

Carefully, we were told: "You must appreciate exactly your circumstances. Think hard. Perhaps you have made a mistake—*if you see what we mean.*"

Then they added: "You would be well advised to give the Red Guards your fullest co-operation. You know, you may have injured this man by accident; and it may be advisable, in your own interests, to explore this line of thought."

That, naturally, is not word perfect; but it is the gist of the British message from Peking.

We decided that we were being guided to make a guarded confession, and we figured that those diplomats knew what was best. It was also clear that there was absolutely nothing they could do for us.

So we typed out two confessions; one in English for the employees of my firm, and one in German for the German company's staff. Their terms were identical. Both statements said that we realized we had injured this man, although it had not been intentional. We apologized for "an unfortunate accident", and hoped that the masses would be generous in their consideration of our case.

At the next meeting with our inquisitors, I was surprised to see the chairman bowing and smiling. I thought, "We've done it."

We were told that the confession of the Germans would be accepted in full, and they would all be discharged. But the British confession could not be accepted.

I blurted out, "But the British confession is exactly the same as the German one."

The reply was cold: "It is not for you to question the decision of the masses. You are being disrespectful to the people. If you carry on like this, you will be in real trouble."

Then we were told to go, and our case would be considered further.

* * *

Back in the hotel that evening, we were badly scared. Crowds had been gathering round the hotel every night, baying like hounds that had scented a crippled fox. Loudspeakers fixed on walls opposite blared out messages of vengeance throughout most of the night. And, as always, the noise of drums, cymbals, and gongs added to the general bedlam.

Few of the Europeans in the Friendship Hotel managed to get more than two or three hours' sleep. And we were worried about the women and children, in case the mob ran riot and invaded the hotel.

Finally, we decided on a desperate gamble. Next day, at the site office, we carried out our plan. I took some old blueprints, and began to burn them outside. Mr. Gin, the interpreter, came running up: "Mr. Watt, what are you doing? Stop at once."

This was the moment. With what I hoped was a theatrical sweep of my arm, I gestured towards some plant which the Russians had been building before they left China six years previously. The buildings were almost in ruins. Grass grew from the roofs. Bushes poked through broken windows, and smashed equipment was scattered all over the place.

"There," I said, "you have so many useless plants that one more won't make any difference. This one might just as well rot, too."

Mr. Gin stared at me. He was angry, and in near panic. I played the Chinese game, and let him sweat for a few minutes. I put another match to the pile.

Looking at him calmly, I said, "I am sure that our company will complain to the Government in Peking about this."

Mr. Gin scurried back to his office, presumably to make an urgent telephone call. I waited, poking at the ashes of the smoldering blueprints.

In a few minutes, he was back, waving his arms and shouting, "Stop, stop, Mr. Watt. We have just had a telephone call from the hospital, and there is wonderful news. The injured man is recovering, and the masses have decided to accept your apology."

I felt the sweat running down the small of my back. I stifled a sigh of relief. At last, somehow, we had managed to find the right raw nerve. For the moment I heard no further word about that firework incident. But it was all dragged up again months later when I was accused of being a spy. The Chinese never forget.

*   *   *

It is interesting that the Chinese accepted the confession of the Lurgi Company of West Germany, but were, to say the least, reluctant to accept the identical confession of the Vickers Company.

I think that this is important, because, at the time, the interpreters made it clear to me that the name of Vickers wasn't entirely unknown. As I've mentioned, I first became aware of this in the Peking War Museum before leaving for Lanchow, and it arose again during the fireworks incident and subsequent trial.

This was my first inkling that the Chinese were not prepared to differentiate between Vickers of armament fame, who had supplied guns to the Chiang Kai Chek government, and Vickers-Zimmer who were manufacturing a synthetic fibre plant. Although I tried to explain the difference, they made it plain that they had no intention of even listening. To the Chinese Communists, there was only one Vickers, and that was that; to them, we were the same old "merchants of death" in another disguise.

They were convinced that any profits which Vickers-Zimmer made would be funnelled back into the pockets of the same shareholders who flourished from the sale of arms.

CHAPTER VII

The Cultural Revolution

The next few months were quiet. It was still early 1967. It now seemed as if the Chinese had never been anything but polite to us. But it was impossible not to feel on edge; they were incomprehensible. One minute they snarled with hate and yelled for your blood; the next, they were all smiles.

I could well appreciate an old Chinese saying which runs: Beware the man who comes to you with a smile. It hides a knife."

But, although they were leaving the Europeans well alone, they were still carrying out mob trials of their own people. One evening, in the Anti-Revisionist Square, I saw two men accused of "giving aid to the enemies of the masses, following deviationist policies and refusing to confess".

Transistor-powered loud hailers were placed first against one ear of each of the men. Red Guards howled through the hailers, blew bugles, whistles, and crashed ear-splitting cymbals until the men collapsed.

They were hauled to their feet, and the hailers switched to the other ear. This was repeated again and again, until finally the men had to be held up. I am sure they were unconscious.

65

Mr. Gin, who had watched all this without a trace of emotion, said to me: "Their punishment is that they should be deafened, so that no more reactionary remarks enter their ears."

By this time, I was beginning to realize that the Chinese will not, as we say in Ireland, call a spoon a spoon or a fork a fork. They have an indirect method of doing things.

Chinese Communists are not very brave, and they have little initiative. They never want to appear conspicuous. But, in numbers, as a mob, the whole attitude changes. They love to get some poor character, put a fool's hat on his head, a rope round his neck, lead him through the streets, put him up on a public platform, and force him to confess.

Slowly, one comes to learn that one must never tell a Chinese Communist that he can possibly make a mistake. He must always be right.

If the victim makes a "good" confession, he'll receive a light punishment. But if he refuses to confess—and I must stress this—they will say that he is not being "honest", and so deserves a "serious punishment". Their official policy—which I heard thousands of times, and even dream about it now—is "Leniency for those who admit their crimes." "Severe punishment for those who stubbornly refuse to do so."

So an innocent man, who has not committed any crime, but is sufficiently cunning, will make some kind of token admission to save his skin.

Returning to the two men deafened by the loud hailers— I discovered that they were "intellectuals" who didn't want to admit to so-called crimes. I was standing against a shop window, and the glass was vibrating with the noise from the hailers, known in the United States as bull horns.

I asked Mr. Gin if he could intercede, and he said, coldly, "No."

Then he gave me another example of the evasive Chinese Communist talk. . . . He referred to the two men as "generals". He said, "The generals are holding out"— meaning that they weren't making their confessions. . . . "The masses are bringing up the big guns to deal with

66

them." (The big guns, the heavy artillery, were the loud hailers.)

Horrified as I was, I was still fascinated by this indirect kind of talk.

On the way back to the hotel Mr. Gin said, "Yes, the generals have put up a strong battle, but the revolutionary masses are winning. Our big guns have blasted the generals into submission. They can't hold out much longer." And more of this evasive military talk.

Funnily enough, a few days later, some Germans from another construction company were leaving to go to Hong Kong on holiday, after being held up by the security police for three months. They said to me, "Paddy, what's happening today?"

And I couldn't resist pulling their legs. I said, "Oh, there's heavy fighting in the town; big battles raging, another great victory for the revolutionary masses. Some generals were stubbornly holding out, but the revolutionary masses brought up heavy artillery and bombarded them into submission."

Mr. Gin was with me, and he nodded approval. . . . "That is exactly what is happening."

I found difficulty in trying not to laugh. And I had almost forgotten about the incident when, about ten days later, I turned on my transistor radio to hear the BBC and the Voice of America. A news reader announced: "Usually reliable sources in Hong Kong have reported that heavy fighting has taken place at Lanchow in Kansu province, between the revolutionary masses and senior army officers who are holding out. It is known that Mao's supporters brought up heavy artillery. . . ."

And he went on to describe details of this bloody battle in Lanchow. I sat there with my eyes popping. I was certainly spreading rumors now, with a vengeance. Doesn't this indicate how, when there are atrocities, nothing is disclosed to the outside world?

I have found that many Western journalists, unaware of this quaint Chinese "indirect" method, have been misled by what they saw. They would read wall posters about big guns and great battles; but in fact, these referred only to a few people being executed or being tortured into making false confessions.

*   *   *

I have indicated that the Chinese are reluctant to accept responsibility. This is too mild a word; they are *terrified* of being held responsible for almost anything. It seems to me to be all part of the insane creed to destroy individualism at all costs.

One could see this in many little instances. For example, we'd send a letter and we just wouldn't get a reply. Week after week would pass, and nothing would happen.

We decided that we'd need to set up a more effective system. So we'd type a letter, and take it by hand to the interpreters' room, with a little book, and ask for a signature of receipt.

This really put the wind up them. We'd leave the letter on the interpreters' table and pass the book along for someone to sign. They would make all kinds of ridiculous excuses. One would perhaps hurry out to the lavatory. If I physically put the receipt book into the hands of one interpreter, he'd quickly give it to a colleague. And so it would go on, like a party game of playing "hot potatoes". No one would take the responsibility of giving a signature for the letter.

They are masters at giving evasive answers, always terrified at being pinned down to something definite—however trivial.

I found that this neurotic fear of appearing in the least bit conspicuous entered into all spheres of their work. When we did get a decision on any point, it was only after long and tedious "group discussions" and long delays.

*   *   *

Little or indeed nothing of the Cultural Revolution has ever been presented to the Western reader. I am writing here for the layman. I do not profess to be an expert on the Cultural Revolution. The full story has not been told— even to the Chinese themselves.

I am, however, conversant with the basic principles, and, in a nutshell, they are as follows:

The Cultural Revolution in China was a struggle between two opposing political lines. One line of thought was presented under the leadership of the Chairman of the Central Committee of the Communist Party, Mao Tsetung. The other, on a completely different line of political thought, was advocated by the President of the People's Republic of China, Liu Shao-Chi.

The President decided that it would be in the interests of the Chinese people, and the economic development of Red China, to follow the new Russian pattern initiated by Khrushchev.

As is commonly known, the Soviet Union stagnated for years after the Communists had seized power towards the end of the First World War. During and after the last war this stagnation continued. The defeated enemies—Germany and Japan—made a tremendous recovery in the economic field; the ordinary people enjoyed a very good standard of living. But the great Soviet Union didn't forge ahead because its policies were based on Stalinist principles.

Khrushchev on the other hand adopted a new line of political thinking which was completely contrary to that practiced by his predecessor, Stalin. Khrushchev's reasoning was that all human beings are not made out of the same mold; some have more natural ability than others. If they are treated absolutely alike, those with ability will say "To Hell, why should I work any harder when I'm not getting anything out of it?"

Khrushchev gave the signal, therefore, for the people to veer away from the old Stalinist principles, and introduce a system whereby those who would work would (within reason) get rewards. There would be no millionaires in the Soviet Union but at least people would be able to see some benefits in return for hard toil. In other words, Khrushchev favored the incentive system. Those who studied at university would get a bigger salary, have better living accommodation, perhaps even own a motor car.

And, since Khrushchev's day, with this previously unheard of freedom for the Soviet people, they have started as a nation to make some headway.

In China, Liu-Shao-Chi recognized this progressive trend in Russia and he advocated that the Chinese should follow suit. For example, he granted small private plots to farmers, rather than having them work on a co-operative basis on communes.

He found that the output under private management increased; it even, on many occasions, trebled.

The President wanted food for the people. This has always been a serious problem for China—too many mouths to feed.

The progressives in the country who were willing to work hard agreed with Liu Shao-Chi's attitude. But the ne'er-do-wells and the lazy, with which every country is cursed, sat back and frittered away their chances, losing the plot of land allocated to them. Then, when they were down on their uppers, they would put up the great Communist call, "We demand our rights."

This was leading to a divided society, a class society; and this state of affairs upset Mao. It disturbed his ideas of the "robotisation" of the Chinese people. It also upset his dreams of practicing his Mao-worshipping cult; and this new-found freedom was beginning to seep through China.

The intellectuals, almost to a man, supported Liu Shao-Chi. Now it is worth noting that most of the intellecuals in China speak a foreign language, mainly English. The reason for this is that Chinese character writing is a peasant form of expression. One either knows the characters or not. The average peasant only knows a few characters. If he wants to write a letter, he must enlist the help of friends, and all will pool their knowledge of the characters. The same applies when he wants to read a letter. They hold it up, and a group will read it aloud.

I noticed this with wall posters and news sheets. A group would stand around and read or chant aloud. No one person could read from start to finish.

The same applied to newspapers. I saw the guards getting the daily newspapers. They would gather round, and then different people would pipe up as they recognized characters—like an organ—whilst others would remain silent when they obviously couldn't recognize the characters.

Sometimes—but not often—everyone would recognize the characters, and they'd all shout out. On other occasions, perhaps just one reader would know some characters, and he or she would announce the meaning to the others.

Reading a newspaper, therefore, is truly a mass job. And no one could seriously suggest that those characters have any place at all in today's world of advanced technology and science.

The Japanese discovered this "character problem" in their early days of industrialization. They decided that they would have to learn a foreign language. They chose German; reasonably, as in those days Germany was already highly advanced industrially.

But the Chinese, on the other hand, plumped for Russian—advised by their so-called intellectuals after the end of the last war. Then they discovered, to their dismay, that they were denied access to Russian technology; so, reluctantly, they adopted English, which had always been fairly widely spoken in China, mainly because of the British and American influence.

It is widely understood now that those Chinese who have been trained to work in the fields of advanced science automatically learn the English language. And this, of course, brings them into contact with foreign literature, which gives them a fairly good picture of what life is like in the Western world.

This, in turn, not unnaturally, causes discontent. It doesn't take a thinking Chinese long to realize that all the political theory they've been taught—even if not entirely unreasonable—is still, basically, only theory.

Like myself they are not interested in theory. They are much more concerned with stark reality; not what might happen, but what, in fact, does happen.

So, because of Liu Shao-Chi's encouragement to the people with ability, and the offer of incentives, most of the intellectuals supported him and opposed Mao.

On the other hand, the peasant masses—especially the

typically Communist ne'er-do-wells who had frittered away their time and wouldn't contribute any hard work, firmly supported Mao.

This set the scene for a tremendous battle for leadership at top level, between Liu Shao-Chi and Mao. It also sparked off a great deal of vicious and barbarous strife between the hard workers and the ne'er-do-wells. In other words, between groups of people prepared to work and try to get on in the world and develop themselves, and all the others who because they themselves were useless and couldn't get anywhere in the world, wanted to drap everyone else into the mire with them.

Mao had a great gift for poetry and with a vast propaganda machine behind him, he appealed to the illiterate masses. He possessed a genius for talking to them in everyday language which, of course, they appreciated. He loved to talk to them in well worn clichés, such as "people who lord it over you", "they ride on your backs"—and he was thus able to whip up the masses to rebel against Liu's intellectuals.

Following Mao's instructions, all hell broke out throughout China.

People who worked in offices and didn't do manual work—doctors, lawyers, all professional people, even those with only a smattering of education—were terrified by the masses.

I myself have watched crazed hordes of illiterates bursting into universities, pulling out professors, beating them up in the street, then putting a fool's cap on their head and a rope round their neck, and parading them through the town.

Some professors, if they were astute enough, would then make their "confessions", standing on a platform in the town square, thanking the masses for "re-educating" them. And those university dons who refused to go along with this would be tortured; and, in some cases, executed.

A surprising aspect of this was that Mao somehow contrived to win the support of young students.

When I thought about it, however, the reason didn't seem too obscure.

It seemed to me that it was simply because many undergraduates the world over have always imagined that they are imbued with the wisdom of the ages, and that they, and they alone, have the ability to put right all the wrongs of the world.

But, thankfully, this "great knowledge" stays with them for only a few years. Once they graduate, and settle into a job, they find that life isn't so bad after all. They become what Communists would describe as "less revolutionary".

So Mao praised the students, closed down the universities, and declared every day a "rag" day. Students were encouraged to run riot, seize their former professors, and "re-educate" them. They would lead the illiterate hordes into government offices, heap files on to a bonfire, and beat up everyone who held responsible positions.

I was there at what was probably the peak of barbarism, and I found that no one with even the slightest veneer of education would be drawn into making a decision.

I have witnessed senior engineers turn around, run off, and hide as soon as they saw us approach—scared that we would ask them a question.

I recall the case of a former chief engineer who failed to show up for a conference with us. He later sent a letter of apology, explaining that he was now relegated to cleaning out the lavatories. He said that he felt conscientiously that he could "better serve the masses" by doing that.

Even the Chinese "fellow travellers" and the Russians were appalled at the barbarism. They accurately described the so-called Cultural Revolution as a reign of terror in which intellectuals were being terrorized by the illiterate hordes.

Mao made no bones about this vulgar, unprincipled struggle for leadership. The Communists know only too well that whoever wants to maintain power must control the army. Fortunately for Mao, his old friend, Lin Piao (later purged), was commander of the army, and President Liu was quickly placed under house arrest.

I have observed from my close study of socialist politics over the years that those with Mao's type of beliefs usually spend their most useful energies engaged in strife with other socialists, who, in their view, have gone a little too far to the left or the right.

The Communists usually use most colorful language to each other; their main descriptions being "traitor" or "scab".

* * *

It was fairly obvious to us, even in 1967, that Liu Shao-Chi was on the losing side, and the Mao gang well in front.

Probably the reason was that Mao's wife—a former film star—was by "coincidence" a leading member of the Central Committee, and in charge of party propaganda. This helped to get Mao off to a flying start, because Mao believes that to win political power it is first necessary to work in what he terms "the ideological sphere". By this is meant "mind conditioning"—or more accurately, brainwashing.

This, then, is the background to the conditions in which we were living in 1967.

By June of that year, the local fighting had died down and I assumed, wrongly as it turned out, that we were over the peak of terror.

CHAPTER VIII

My Wife's Visit

The hatred of the Chinese could be directed against anything and everything. During my early weeks in Lanchow there were demonstrations against the Americans, Indians, Indonesians, and Japanese. So it did not surprise me overmuch when I found that we were in "British week".

This was sparked off when Chinese nationals, living and working in Hong Kong as reporters for the Communist Press, decided to extend their activities to taking part in riots. The Chinese government was greatly disturbed when the Hong Kong authorities ruled that this sort of behavior was not permissible.

Naturally, the small group of British subjects in the atomic city of Lanchow had to bear the brunt of local wrath.

We watched from our hotel windows as tens of thousands of angry Chinese streamed past the gates, looking up at us, and shaking their fists. They beat drums, waved flags, and chanted anti-British slogans. At the time, I don't think we took it too seriously, our attitude tended to be—let us lie low for a while; next week, perhaps tomorrow, it will be the turn of some other country to top the Hate Parade.

But after a few days of this non-stop bedlam, we decided to return to work as usual, in our bus.

As we drew up to the office block, we saw a large crowd of Chinese gathered around the door. I had the uncomfortable feeling that we were in for a rough passage; the mob looked as if they were about to vent some of their pent-up passions.

Suddenly they stampeded—like steers in a Hollywood Western—all trying to squeeze in through the office doors. It was a fantastic sight; one movement we had an unruly mob; the next, not one Chinese was to be seen.

Then I looked up. Every window in the entire office block was crammed with staring faces.

Then we saw what it was all about—slogans. Scrawled all over the walls and doors were anti-British slogans . . . "The British Imperialists Owe the Chinese a Debt which must be paid in *blood*, no matter how long it takes."

But, obviously, by their behavior they did not feel like debt collecting that day.

We walked along and looked into a ground-floor window. All the faces disappeared immediately. We went to the next window; again the faces vanished.

I could only conclude that we had interrupted their slogan scrawling. They were bold enough to paint up abuse of the British, but lacked the courage to say anything to our faces. Once again, it was the typical action of the evasive Chinese Communist.

* * *

Their outburst of anti-British hysteria took place in May 1967, but this had died down by early June and the Chinese once again seemed disposed to be friendly.

75

I felt that it would be safe for me to go ahead with plans to have my wife visit me for a two-month holiday. First, I talked it over with Mr. Gin. He was most co-operative ... "Certainly, they will be welcome."

I knew that some of the British diplomats in Peking had their wives and children with them. Here in Lanchow one of the British families had a small boy, and there were three or four German children. And, after all, my family were not entirely unused to foreign travel. They had been with me for most of my stay in West Africa.

I decided to let them join me. What a mistake I made. . . .

*   *   *

Their journey from London followed the normal course; they had been delayed in Peking while they waited for their connection to Lanchow.

I remember standing at Lanchow airport, watching the tiny, Russian-built Aleutian aircraft circling overhead, knowing that it was bringing my wife and children to me and that, with luck, I'd be speaking to them in a few minutes' time.

I say "with luck", because at that time all visitors to China were met by a welcoming committee who set up an infernal din with fanatical Red Guards screaming quotations from Mao's Thoughts, and using every instrument imaginable to make a noise.

When I rushed over to meet Josephine and the children I couldn't make myself heard. And she shouted back in my ear, not words of love, but an unbelieving, "George, this is *bedlam*." All I could do was nod.

I bundled them into the taxi, and we set off for Lanchow, this ancient walled city on the banks of the Yellow River where it passes through a mountain range. It was built many centuries before London, and here tolls were collected from the camel trains coming from the north.

Lanchow airport—or, correctly, rough landing strip—is at the base of a mountain which rises almost perpendicularly about two miles south-east of the city. So the taxi had to pass through the city walls, crawl slowly through the densely populated mud streets, and out again through the west gate to the Friendship Hotel.

As was customary, the manager was waiting on the steps to greet new arrivals. But to my amazement this wasn't the manager I knew. It was an old man who normally looked after the garden. Solemnly, he was introduced as the new manager. The staff explained, through the interpreter, that they had been studying Mao's pronouncements about turning things upside down. So they decided to make the hotel manager the gardener, and the gardener the manager. I just couldn't take this in, and I think my wife really thought she had arrived in an Alice in Wonderland set-up.

It transpired that the hotel staff had seized the manager, beaten him up, put the usual fool's hat on his head, and led him with a rope around his neck on a parade of the hotel corridors. Crowds followed the wretched man, beating gongs and cymbals. The British and German wives, alone in the hotel, as their husbands were still at work, were completely terrified.

The staff then drove the deposed manager outside and put him to work in the greenhouse. Sure enough, that evening, walking round the back of the hotel, I saw this unfortunate man down on his knees, weeding. He looked up at me with two of the most prominent black eyes I have ever seen.

I tried to explain to Jo—not very successfully—that it was all part of the Cultural Revolution; and that things which didn't happen in civilized countries were accepted as normal in China.

The first practical problem was that my wife and children couldn't sleep at night for the noise. Opposite the hotel was the headquarters of the Party or, rather, one of its factions. All night long loudspeakers on the flat roof blared out anti-Imperialist slogans. As I had been in Lanchow since the previous December I'd become used to the noise, although I admit it was like living right inside Grand Central Station, New York.

There was little really for the family to do. But it was

my practice to retain one of the three taxis in Lanchow, so I took them shopping. In China, as in Russia, shops operate on a different pattern from stores in Britain. They work a shift system, open from early morning till late evening.

But the shops were poor. It was obvious, even to my inexperienced eye that food was scarce, indeed that there was a famine in the area. My wife, incidentally, had a ratio-exemption card, given to most foreigners; but the quality of goods, particularly clothing, was so shoddy that we didn't bother to buy anything.

About this time, an incident happened that caused me trouble later when I was being interrogated by security police.

I was reading from the propaganda sheets given foreigners about "bumper harvests". It was obvious that there was, to put it mildly, a serious scarcity of food. Casually, I mentioned to a shopkeeper through the interpreter that the crops seemed to be extremely poor. But to demonstrate how kind the Chinese are—from his point of view—he conceded: "Yes, that is so; but we have just had two bags of rice flown in specially for the foreign technicians."

I pointed out that this wasn't necessary, and added that we were sorry if it left the local people short. Immediately, the interpreter screamed at the shopkeeper, and a tremendous row broke out. It was much later that I discovered I had posed "loaded questions to try to find out about the economic situation". That is just a small example of how a casual remark from a foreigner—always under suspicion—can be wrongly interpreted.

* * *

One evening I stood aghast for a full minute on the landing leading to my hotel room. I couldn't move. I couldn't say a word. I just stared over the banister.

There, directly below me, was the huge, gold-leafed bust of Mao Tse-tung mounted on an 8ft-high pedestal. But the head was now smothered with the pulp, juice, and pips of a tomato which had landed smack on top of it.

My wife, who hadn't seen what happened, pushed me

gently in the back: "George, what's the matter?" I said nothing. How could I tell her that our little boy, Steven, then not quite two, had just insulted the leader of 700 million people—at a time when any remark could set the Red Guards on the rampage?

We had stopped at the hotel shop to buy fruit, and Steven was carrying a ripe tomato.

I hadn't noticed Steven scrambling up the stairs ahead of us. Stopping to peer through the banister halfway up the second flight, he dropped the tomato. It rolled through the rails and plopped on to the golden head below.

I groaned to myself, "Stevie, what have you started now?" I had visions of my son being hauled before a Red Guards trial and told to confess. Confess? He had only justed started speaking his first few words!

I routed out Mr. Gin and the hotel staff, pointed to the head of Mao then to Steven, trying by sign language to assure them that it had been an accident. Mr. Gin was furious. I said over and over again, "My little boy . . . It was an accident. He is only a baby. He did not mean any harm."

Then I stood on a chair beneath Mao's bust, and, with a handkerchief, carefully wiped away every trace of that tomato. I don't think that golden head ever shone so brightly before.

Gradually I managed to placate Mr. Gin and the staff. They finally seemed to accept my apologies and even gave me a little bow as I left. But I was still apprehensive. My wife was curious. She watched me quietly and I could sense that she was wondering if this was the same man she had kissed goodbye in England some months before.

I said lamely, "This isn't quite like being back home. One has to be a little more careful here."

I didn't want to tell her that the apparent return to normal conditions in Lanchow, which had encouraged me to have the family join me, had been broken only a day or two before she arrived. There had been fighting to the east of the city. We had heard rumors, but deliberately asked no questions, hoping to make it clear that we had no wish to be involved in China's internal politics.

Work at the site had been stopped, and we had been told to stay in the hotel for a few days. It was sticky weather, with the temperature in the 90's.

One afternoon, strolling in the hotel courtyard, we heard the rumble of heavy traffic outside. We looked through the gates, and saw a parade of grey, open lorries packed with Red Guards carrying home-made spears.

There must have been 50 vehicles. They trundled along about 20ft apart at about five miles an hour. Across the radiator of each truck was lashed a human being. Some trucks had two people roped across. All had been spread-eagled diagonally, and tied down with wire or rope.

Other captives, in groups of two, three, or four, had been strapped to the backs or roofs of each driving cab. They drooped helplessly as Red Guards pushed and prodded them. They were young and old, women as well as men. Some had been wounded. Many were in a state of complete collapse.

Those slumped over a driving cab were sometimes grabbed by the hair so that the agonized face was lifted into full view of the screaming crowds lining the road.

There was nothing we could do. I was gripped by the feeling of utter helplessness which I was to experience so many times in my years in China.

As we turned to go back into the hotel, Mr. Gin appeared. He must have seen the disgust on my face. He said, "The masses do not arrest innocent people. They have been ferreting out class enemies of the people, and now they will deal with them."

*   *   *

One day, all the Europeans at the hotel were invited to go swimming in a pool about four miles away on the opposite bank of the Yellow River.

Most were delighted. Jo said, "That would be wonderful, especially for the children."

But I said, "No, we're not going. They are up to something. I don't know what. But I'm certain they're planning to use it in some way for some purpose of their own.

80

Those people *never* give anything away without some strings attached. And this offer is too sudden."

A few of the Europeans, however, did accept. They returned two hours later saying that, although the pool water had not been too clean, it had been very refreshing. The biggest surprise of all was that the police had kept away the crowds of onlookers who always gathered to watch the "long noses".

After dinner that evening we were told that the pool was to be cleaned and filled with fresh water. It would be ready if we would like to make up another swimming party for the day after tomorrow.

This time a much larger group planned to go, but I was still suspicious. Despite the pleas of my family I refused to budge.

It was a happy group of Europeans who went off that morning. They pulled my leg as they left, saying, "You're far too edgy, George. You're at the stage of seeing spooks."

When they returned it had gone nine o'clock and they were furious. They were also hungry. They had had no lunch or dinner—not even a drink of water for the children with them.

At first, they told me, everything had gone well. The pool, as promised, had been refilled with clean water. The crowds had again been kept away, and for about an hour our party had a splendid time.

Then from a distance came a murmur of noise. Thousands of Chinese were running towards the pool, cheering, smiling, and waving. Hundreds of them jumped into the pool, fully clothed, and played and splashed around like children. No attempt was made to harm our party. But they found it unnerving to be the center of attraction for a mob in such a high state of excitement.

The Europeans headed for the rooms where they had left their clothes. . . . The doors were locked. The interpreter, who had the keys, had disappeared.

There was nothing they could do. They stood there for two hours, surrounded by Chinese who, full of curiosity as usual, kept touching their white skins, feeling the texture of the swimming costumes, and staring at the breasts of the women. There was nothing intentionally unpleasant in this curiosity. Most Chinese women tend to be flat-chested, and European women were consequently constantly objects of interest.

The interpreter reappeared as suddenly as he had vanished. The group, hurriedly dressing, made for the bus to return to the hotel. But, on the bridge over the Yellow River, the bus stopped without warning.

The interpreter merely said, "The bus has broken down." Then both he and the driver disappeared. Again the waving crowds gathered, surrounding the bus, tapping the windows, and cheering. They kept this up for nearly an hour. Then, as the Chinese appeared to be so friendly, they decided to walk back to the hotel.

They were about to set out when the interpreter returned to say, "It is impossible to repair the bus. We shall go back to the hotel by river launch."

Although tired and fed up, this apparent show of consideration cheered the Europeans. They boarded the launch readily. But the game was not over yet.

The launch took more than two hours to cover the two miles to the hotel. It hugged the river bank all the way. Sometimes it turned back for a few hundred yards before heading once again for the hotel. Almost every yard of the river bank was lined with cheering, waving crowds, 10 and 12 deep. One of the German engineers said on his return, "It was incomprehensible. It had no meaning, no reason, Yet we had the impression that the crowds were giving us the equivalent of a standing ovation."

Next morning, on the bus taking us to the site, we found out what it was all about.

Mr. Gin produced the morning newspaper, and translated a story which appeared on Page One.

"Class enemies," he intoned solemnly, "have been spreading false rumors that the foreigners at the Friendship Hotel do not hold Chairman Mao in high esteem, and do not recognize him as their leader.

"The foreigners were highly indignant when they heard about this, and freely decided to participate in the celebrations marking the first anniversary of Chairman Mao's swim in the Yangtse River.

"The foreigners, refusing to dress, remained in their swimming costumes for hours as a token of respect. They refused to return to the hotel for lunch or dinner, and requested that the journey should be made by river launch so that they could clearly be seen by the people to be holding Chairman Mao in the highest esteem."

Our friends had been duped and manipulated for propaganda purposes. The only satisfaction was that, for the moment, anyway, the Chinese seemed to want to be friendly.

But this didn't last for long. In about ten days' time there was another burst of anti-British feeling in Lanchow which, I believe, was sparked off by the Communist-inspired troubles in Hong Kong.

Posters reviling "the Imperialist British" were plastered over the walls of the Friendship Hotel. Loudspeakers mounted on a building opposite maintained the messages of hate for 18, 20, and sometimes 24 hours a day. Mr. Gin was always willing to translate, but the message was the same, over and over again. We were "the enemies of the people, the opponents of Mao"—and the Chinese were the only people in the world who were always right. Occasionally, those tirades were interrupted by Chinese music—anything to maintain the volume of noise and prevent the Imperialist long noses from getting their sleep.

Next day the hotel was surrounded by threatening mobs of Red Guards. I was told by one interpreter, who seemed a little embarrassed, "We have got to do this. It is not you personally, you understand."

Intended or not, tension was building. There was no physical violence against us, but the situation was extremely edgy.

The Chinese had troubles of their own, which kept them from concentrating their hate on us. From the snippets of information we heard, we gathered that China was being swept by a reign of terror.

We were in the middle of the furious battle for power

between Mao Tse-tung and his one-time friend, President Liu Shao-Chi.

God knows what went on in the rest of China, but I saw enough mindless savagery in Lanchow to sicken me. Tens of thousands of workers had been drafted in to work on the vast complex of plants outside the city. They were looked on as strangers, and resented by most of the city folk. It was a ready-made situation for a fight.

To add to the tension, food was becoming short. We Europeans managed to get much the same food as before, but we noticed that the Chinese who ate in the hotel restaurant were served mainly with noodles. They did not even get rice.

The food shortage became so severe that the peasants hid much of their produce in mountain caves instead of giving it to the State. The explosion came when some site workers, discovering one of the food caches, killed six or seven peasants.

In the next few days, I watched with mesmerized fascination the preparations for a civil war.

* * *

One day (in August 1967), anvils were set up outside our bedroom windows, and I saw the locals manufacturing spears. When I went to the plant site I found workers cutting up small-bore piping into six-foot lengths to use as spear shafts. This was piping that had already been fitted and installed. I went almost berserk. I yelled at them, "Are you crazy? Those pipes are the arteries of this site. . . . If you cut them out, you kill this site."

Their answer was to brandish their ever-present red books, and tell me that they were acting "according to the Thoughts of Mao".

I was so furious that I shouted, "Forget his bloody thoughts. It's about time you listened to *my* thoughts."

They paid no attention. They carried on, fashioning the lengths of pipe into crude spears by lashing screwdrivers, chisels, and other sharp tools to the ends.

Returning to the hotel, I saw hundreds of people making

large blocks out of mud, stone, and concrete. They used them to block up the shop doors and ground-floor windows of their homes. Every building was being turned into a fortress. The flat roofs of the buildings were being loaded up with stones—hauled up in baskets. Rope ladders dangled from upper-story windows.

Later that night we heard the noise of metal being hammered. In the back courtyard of the hotel was an anvil and a portable charcoal forge; around them were the hotel waiters and cooks, and they, too, were making spears. Broom handles and lengths of bamboo were being used for shafts, and the heads were being fashioned from the tops of nearby railings. Some merely had kitchen knives and forks lashed to the ends.

This do-it-yourself weapon-making went on for some days until one morning, about four o'clock, we were awakened by the most terrible screaming . . . drums beating, shouting, cymbals crashing. From the bedroom windows we could see fires on the outskirts of the city. It began to die down, and, just on first light, there was silence. Clearly, it would be no use our going to the site that day. But I was sick with another worry. I remembered seeing the workers pulling parts of our plant to bits. I had visions of the plant being smashed, and this would mean that I should have to stay in China for another year or more.

So I persuaded Mr. Gin to accompany me. We went in a taxi, and about halfway on the six-mile journey we ran into a battle. Hundreds of Chinese were fighting across the roadway, and we were caught in a cross-fire of sniping. Mr. Gin and I got out and ran to a ditch. We were pinned there for more than an hour until the battle moved on towards the city. We made a dash for the taxi and reached the site.

Some workers were still making spears. They surrounded us, and, to my amazement, Mr. Gin told me they were asking if I would help them.

He added, "The situation is not as bad as it looks."

I couldn't see any reason in this.

I replied, "To my mind, the situation is *exactly* as it

85

looks. I'm not interested in politics. I'm only interested in the welfare of the plant."

Then the political commissar said, "Incidentally, there is a little job you could do for us—tell us how to increase the temper in some metals, and how to reduce it in brittle metal—such as files are made of—so that it won't snap too easily when used in a spear head."

I didn't argue. I just stood there, and gave them an hour's course of instruction. It was the strangest job I'd ever done in my life, standing at a blacksmith's forge, surrounded by hundreds of young students, industrial workers—and, of course, Red Guards—showing them how to manufacture highly tempered spear heads.

After some hours, they agreed I could leave; and I was certainly thankful. As I left I said sarcastically that I must arrange for Vickers to send them the latest catalogue of spears so that they would not have to damage the site any more.

For once they saw the joke and there was a roar of laughter.

When I got back to the hotel all my colleagues gathered round. They looked at me as if I had just returned from outer space; they said they hadn't expected to see me alive again.

During the next few days nothing happened. The political commissar called the senior engineers together, told us that they thought the main battles were over, and suggested that some volunteers should go to the site and collect drawings, blueprints, and other valuable documents and instruments, and bring them back to the hotel for safe keeping.

So a few of us went to the site by bus and loaded our stuff into crates. Then, just as we were about to leave, some grim-faced political commissars arrived and announced that we could not leave the industrial area. It seemed that while we were in the area the workers had left in lorries, and were now attacking the town, where our wives and children were. We were all now sick with worry and imagined all kinds of appalling things, since we knew the lengths to which those people were prepared to go.

As darkness fell it was decided that we should go back into the bus, and enter the town after making a detour. It worked. But once we had returned to the safety of the hotel, we heard the full story of what had happened that afternoon. My wife told me that she had gone with some other women and the children up to the flat roof of the hotel because they thought they would be safer up there; there were so many doors they could lock behind them, and even if it was not one hundred per cent safe, at least it was better than staying on the ground floor. They stood watching the bloody battle below as the workers, armed with spears, pushed the residents back. This went on hour after hour until the road was strewn with bodies.

Young Christine—aged eight—had a hysterical fit of sobbing when she saw the mob surround a man and plunge their crude javelins and spears into him until he fell in a twisting heap of spurting blood.

For two or three days the battles went on. Dead and injured lay all over the place. During a lull I made a dash for the shop at the hotel entrance to get some supplies, including sweets for the children and beer for us. The shop was wrecked. The old man who ran it, a spear driven right through his stomach, was suspended in the space of the counter-flap by the ends of the spear being placed on both sides of the counter. He had at one time owned the shop and, after the Communist revolution, had been allowed to remain as manager.

I knew then that I had to get my family out of this crazed country. They couldn't go on taking this kind of thing much longer, and I couldn't just stand by watching their misery.

I appealed to the commissars to let my family and myself leave the area, so that I could see them out of China, and perhaps spend a few days with them in the adjoining British colony of Hong Kong before they flew back to Britain and civilization. I, of course, had no choice but to return to Lanchow and help finish the construction of the plant.

CHAPTER IX

The Sacking of the Peking Mission

On 18 August, 1967, an event in China made headline news throughout the world. . . . Two hundred Red Guards smashed into the home of Anthony Grey, Reuter's correspondent in Peking, and imprisoned him in his home for 26 tortuous months in solitary confinement.

Anthony Grey later became my friend, and inscribed a copy of his book, *Solitary, in China,*[1] to me—"To George Watt who survived a rough time in an inimitable Irish way. Good luck."

On page 70 of his book he writes significantly of an event which happened just five days after my wife and family arrived:

> "My spirits sank further when on July 17 another New China News Agency demonstration at the British Mission was laid on after two more of their Hong Kong reporters were arrested. Several hundred Chinese hurled rotten tomatoes and stones at the two British diplomats who went to the gate to receive their petition."

This was one of the Chinese anti-British weeks—or just Hate Weeks. They would stop work, stream through the streets, foaming at the mouth, their eyes bulging—as if their batteries had been newly charged with some form of high powered hate. After a few days of this they would settle down again to work until the bottled-up hate resurged once more. They were really like batteries; they needed a political charge to inspire them to do a little bit of work, then they would slow down to almost stop. Under these circumstances they were unpredictable. Suddenly, they would discover that some other nation had upset

---

[1] *Solitary, in China* by Anthony Grey (Michael Joseph— £2.00).

China and off they would go on another screaming match.

The Chinese Communists are unable to maintain continuity of work. They will almost invariably carry out a section of a project, then stop while they plan and study for a week; back to complete another section, and again another stop. They will continue like this *ad infinitum*.

So we had this stop-and-start industrial pattern—working for a little, then stopping for study—inside a stop-and-start political pattern.

* * *

Eventually, on 22 August, we were permitted to leave Lanchow for Peking, where we had booked in at the Hsin Chao hotel. I remember sitting on the edge of the bed, saying to my wife, "Thank God, at last we are on our way out now—safe."

Little did I know that 22 August was to be a turning point in my life.

Our happiness at landing safely in Peking was to last for only a few moments.

I had my Grundig transistor radio with me. I noticed that it was on the hour, and tuned into London to catch the BBC news, on their General Overseas Service. The first item absolutely stunned us—the British Mission in Peking was in flames. It was under seige by Red Guards, with the British diplomats trapped inside. It had been attacked only hours before. The message had been relayed from Singapore.

There I was, sitting in a hotel only a few hundred yards away.

Jo, her face showing strain, whispered, "George, George . . . will we ever get away now?"

I put my arms round her, and tried to soothe her. One thing I knew for certain—I could not dismiss this with a shrug, and say, "Oh, to hell, let them roast." Part of my undoing was that perhaps I too had been brain-washed a little bit.

As a native of Northern Ireland, I am British. From

childhood, I had been indoctrinated—brainwashed, if you like—to believe how wonderful it is to be British. And to an Ulster Unionist it is very important to be British. So, on that day in Peking, I couldn't just turn away and say that it was none of my business. As a Briton, I was *involved*.

My idea was to try to smuggle some wives and children out of the diplomats' married quarters, and lodge them in the comparative safety of the hotel.

I avoided the interpreter as I put Jo and the children into a taxi. We decided it would be best to keep together. I knew a few words of Chinese, and was able to give instructions to the driver.

I knew my way to the diplomatic compound, as I had stayed in Peking for a few days on my way to Lanchow. We stopped on the far side of the married quarters, a block of flats built in a rectangle around an enclosed courtyard.

I knew that I wasn't exaggerating the danger, because on my last visit to Peking I had seen a little child murdered by the Red Guards. I had no illusions about what those monsters were capable of doing.

Leaving the family in the taxi, I entered the courtyard, and came out about 50 yards from the Mission building. It was still smoldering. Around it, dancing, capering, yelling, and screaming, were thousands of Chinese. Among them were a few Europeans, some who have since been identified as British subjects. Yes, British citizens—Communists, fellow travellers of the Chinese—actually took part in the attack on the Mission.

As I was in shirtsleeves and without a tie, I felt fairly sure that, with luck, the mob wouldn't identify me as a diplomat, and might ignore me. Mingling with the crowd as casually as possible, I edged slowly in towards the Mission. It was a successful bluff.

As I pushed through. I would occasionally wave a clenched fist. and yell. "Up the Irish." When I spotted any Chinese eyeing me with suspicion, I'd nod and wink as if we were the best of comrades—and push on. Not very bright, perhaps, but it was the best I could think of at the time.

When I eventually reached the building itself, it looked completely destroyed. I felt sure that if anyone remained inside, they couldn't possibly be alive.

So I carefully zig-zagged back through that heaving crowd until I got to the taxi. Jo looked scared out of her wits. I had been away for more than an hour.

Telling the taxi to wait, I went to the gable end of the diplomatic block where I'd been told the British had taken refuge. Upstairs, at the end of a corridor, I came to a door with a little Union Jack painted on it. Below it, scrawled on a scrap of paper, I read: "New Office, British Chargé d'Affaires".

When I knocked, the door was opened by a tall man; beside him was an unsheathed dress sword. I thought, "I wouldn't like to be the first Red Guard through this door."

Suddenly, I knew I was looking at a familiar face. He immediately recognized me, but couldn't place my name.

I said to him, "Where's your watch?" He looked at his bare wrist. That jolted his memory. . . .

Three years earlier, in August 1964, I had been returning home from Nigeria. I was on my final leave and, because I had so much heavy luggage, I went by sea. The journey from Lagos to Liverpool took about two weeks.

On the second day out on the journey north, we stopped at Takoradi in Ghana to pick up passengers for the United Kingdom. I noticed one man in particular as he came on board—a tall, spare, military looking figure.

During the journey home we became great friends. He was in the British High Commission in Ghana. At Las Palmas in the Canary Islands we went ashore together. I took him to where he could buy a duty-free watch—an Omega Seamaster. He was so proud of it.

When we parted at Liverpool, the last thing I told him was, "See that you don't lose that watch. . . ."

And now, three years later, here was my old friend from Ghana. But now minus his watch. The Red Guards had stolen it.

* * *

It was a pleasant reunion with my British diplomat friend, but, unfortunately, he and his colleagues had a sorry tale to tell. When the Chinese attacked, Sir Donald Hopson, the Chargé d'Affaires, organized the staff, and said: "We shall go out in a block, with the women in the middle." He led the escape bid himself. But the group was scattered almost as soon as it came through the front door. Sir Donald was grabbed and told to bow. He refused, and they forced him to his knees.

The girl secretaries were seized by the ankles, and dragged down the steps. Some were assaulted in a vile manner. One of them was rescued by an elderly Chinese policeman who, pushing her into the back of his little sentry box, stood at the entrance to beat off the mob with his truncheon.

Everyone said that Sir Donald had been magnificent; how fortunate they were to be led by such a brave man.

The group was saved from further violence by the diversionary tactics of the First Commercial Secretary, Alastair Hunter. Thinking that the married quarters might also be attacked, it had been arranged that he should stay behind that morning in case he could do anything for the wives and children in an emergency. He watched the attack on the Mission from a window and when he saw his colleagues being dragged out, he locked all the women and children in a room, told them to keep quiet, and hurried to a side entrance of the flats.

Once in the street, he used himself as bait to attract the attention of the mob. As they turned, he started running in the opposite direction. It was just enough o divert their energies, and the battered diplomats scrambled for the flats. Alastair was able to shake off his pursuers and join his colleagues.

One disgusting incident they told me about concerned the behavior of some women Red Guards. They had taken great delight—and caused amusement among the crowd—in seizing some male diplomats by their private parts.

There I was, the first British subject on the scene; and,

although some of my compatriots had been seriously beaten up, I was relieved to find them still alive. It made me feel proud to be with them. I did what I could to cheer them up and make them comfortable.

But when I returned to my hotel, I was met by a group of interpreters who screamed at me: "Filthy Imperialist dog! You have dared to render aid to British diplomats. You deserve the same punishment that they have received."

I didn't answer. I just walked past them, up to the bedroom where my wife and children were sitting.

Within minutes, I was summoned into the corridor by officials. I anticipated a ticking off for having dared to leave the hotel without the interpreter.

I wish it had been only that. A stream of abuse was unleashed. One of them stabbed his finger at me, and his words struck a chill to my heart. . . . "You Imperialist lackey. . . . You have not heard the last of this. There are no seats on the aircraft tomorrow for you or your family. You are ALL to stay in Peking until further notice."

So, by helping the diplomats, I had now involved my family—who were expecting to fly to Canton in the morning to catch the train for Hong Kong. We were now held under arrest in Peking. I was filled with dread, but there was nothing we could do. We just continued to live in the hotel, the days passing drearily by.

Sometimes we went out to the park opposite. The public took little notice of us, because there were so many foreign visitors in Peking, and one couldn't distinguish between British, French, and Germans. In that, we were quite safe. Occasionally, Red Guards would suddenly appear, blowing whistles. This meant that everyone had to stop and gather round them. Red books were produced, and the contents read out; they were, of course, *The Thoughts of Chairman Mao*. These thoughts, incidentally, were altered from time to time, as some "thoughts" were found not to be so suitable, after all.

After a reading session of perhaps ten or fifteen minutes, the Red Guards would blow their whistles again. Everyone would then put away their red books and continue on their way. This was indeed mass discipline. No one would dare to walk on until the whistles were blown. And this performance went on at least once every hour during the day.

For two weeks, I lived a cat-and-mouse existence with Mr. Shah, the interpreter. Whenever I asked when we would be permitted to leave, he smiled, and with sinister politeness, said, "Perhaps today. Perhaps tomorrow . . . you cannot escape. The people have long memories. They will never forget, nor forgive. We now have a more detailed report of your activities against the Chinese people, and the Red Guards are very angry. . . ."

Once, I said to him, "You are, of course, Mr. Shah, speaking only about me?"

"No," he replied, "we mean your family also."

I protested that they surely couldn't beat up a woman and two children.

"Oh yes, we can," he snapped. "You are all British, and the British owe us a debt—blood debts—since 1842. Those debts must be paid for in blood. . . ."

He was referring to the Anglo-Chinese Treaty of 1842 which handed Hong Kong over to the British.

The Chinese never ceased to astonish me.

"But that happened 125 years ago," I said.

"It matters not," said Mr. Shah, "how long it takes. A crime must be put right in the end. The debt must be paid."

By the tenth day of that fortnight, I had endured about all I could take. After dinner that night, Jo and the children stayed in the locked room while I went upstairs to the bar.

There was a group of African soldiers in the far corner, perhaps about fifty in all. This interested me, on account of the years I had spent in Africa.

They were mainly from Tanzania and Zambia. They told me quite openly that they were "Freedom Fighters", then in China to be trained as guerrillas to operate in South Africa.

I had a drink or two with them, but I never realized that evening that I was under observation, that I would

94

be reported for trying to steal important military intelligence.

There was also a bunch of Australians and New Zealanders, all confirmed Maoists. One of them slapped me on the back and invited me to have some brandy. I don't drink much, and seldom touch spirits, but I was so depressed that I had four or five Chinese brandies—made, I think, from bananas. That, I'm afraid, loosened my tongue.

I had been listening to the Australians singing the praises of Mao, and how they were returning to Australia to "tell the truth about the new China". I should explain that most of the Communists in Australia and New Zealand follow the Maoist pattern rather than the Soviet philosophy which is followed in most Westernised countries. This group was what I'd call "One-week experts". They had visited China several times, but their knowledge of China was restricted to what their hosts chose to show them on carefully conducted tours. Of course, in their opinion, and like most China visitors, they then regarded themselves as infallible authorities on China.

I said bitterly, "Yes, that's a splendid idea. Tell the world the truth about China. Tell them about the heavy fighting in Lanchow. . . . Tell them that the Chinese are holding my wife and children hostage in Peking, and have threatened to beat them up."

But they refused to believe me. One Australian girl said, "Surely you are not seriously suggesting that the Chinese would do such terrible things?"

"You are their friends," I answered, "why don't you ask them yourselves."

Next morning, in the lift to the breakfast room, I met one of the group, an Australian woman in her early sixties, who had spent her childhood in my native Ireland. She whispered in my ear, "Don't worry. We are working for you. I think your wife and children will soon be able to leave."

Could I trust her? I wanted to, desperately. But she was a Maoist. Perhaps they had roped her in to pour another drop of poison on my mental agony.

95

After breakfast, some members of the previous night's group came over to my table. One said, in a soft voice, "We have appealed to the Chinese on your behalf. We have explained to them that it is not the custom in Western countries to carry out reprisals against women or children. We have pleaded with them, in the name of international friendship. They will make a decision this morning."

I found it gratifying that those Commonwealth Communists were prepared to put the principles of civilized conduct before their political dogma.

In an hour or so, a political commissar invited me to a room along the corridor where a group of Chinese were assembled. Then he announced: *"We* have decided that your wife and children may leave the country. But you are to remain behind."

I was fascinated by his emphasis on *"We"*, for I knew very well that it was the well-meaning fellow travellers who had been instrumental in securing the release of my wife and children.

Two days later, the interpreter knocked on the hotel room door early in the morning. I woke up, thinking it was the Red Guards bursting in. Then I remembered the conversation in the corridor. Even at that moment I thought "I wonder if this is really genuine at last or whether they have decided we have committed further crimes."

This time it was indeed true. Mr. Shah stood outside, impassively. He said crisply: "Your wife and children must pack their bags. They will leave for the airport at noon tomorrow."

I couldn't believe the news. I think we were too stunned to be ecstatic. The first thing I did was to telephone Alastair Hunter at the Mission. They knew that some French diplomats were also leaving Peking, and they arranged that these friends would accompany my wife and children to Shanghai, then on by Air France to Paris. The strain under which everyone had been existing in Communist China had helped to weld all diplomats together, irrespective of nationality.

How well I remember that departure.

It was 5 September, 1967. I accompanied my family on to the tarmac. I can see my wife standing on the steps of the aircraft, her eyes swimming with tears; and little Steven calling out, "Daddy . . . Daddy."

In that moment I felt that I'd never see my family again. I was certain that I was being roped into something evil. This was not only an international incident; I was sure I was now engulfed in a wave of terror. It is difficult to explain the situation, because this was something that could not possibly happen in the Western world.

No doubt, one could point to the theories of that great "humanitarian", Karl Marx; but I am not interested in what *should* happen. I am reporting something which is starkly true.

Here I was on my own in Communist China.

I felt terribly alone—and doomed.

I watched the little aircraft take off, and followed its track until it was a tiny speck in the eastern sky, and finally vanished. With a tremendous feeling of relief I told myself that my family were at last on their way to the free and civilized world.

As I walked back to the taxi, my step was light. A burden had gone from my shoulders.

In the hall of the hotel sat the fellow travellers—Maoists from Australia, New Zealand, Canada, Britain—the one-week "experts" who were returning to their various countries to tell the "truth" about Communist China.

They were celebrating because, as one of them said, "The great Chinese people will be for ever friendly with the great Australian people." They all used the word "great" so often that I immediately recognized they had been imbued with the Chinese style. As I mentioned earlier, the Chinese so freely use the word *"Da"* meaning "great"; "big"): naturally, fellow travellers quickly pick it up in conversation.

CHAPTER X

Alone in Peking

That evening I telephoned the office of the British Chargé d'Affaires in Peking. I was told something which caused me distress but, at the same time, a measure of satisfaction, too.

When my wife left Peking for Shanghai, she had to join an Air France flight for Europe. The British Mission had asked our French diplomat friends on the aircraft to keep an eye on my wife and children, and see that they had a comfortable and safe journey. It was thought that the Chinese might molest them, or at least subject them to some form of abuse.

When my wife arrived in Shanghai she was seized by Customs officials, and, with the children, hustled to a corner of the inspection area. In full view of everyone, she was almost completely stripped, and all her belongings searched. Then she was kept standing around for several hours. The children were so exhausted that they just lay down on the cold concrete and fell asleep.

Some passengers wanted to go to her help, but they were ordered to go away.

The Chinese searched her handbag, and discovered that she had a few cents over the amount of currency she had declared. The amount would be equal to a British penny. But the Communists said they weren't concerned with the actual sum, trivial as it was; what mattered was "principal". A penny over the stated amount should be treated no differently to one thousand pounds excess. They insisted that she had committed "serious currency offenses".

The other passengers were ordered to board the aircraft. My wife was told that she would remain behind, to be placed on trial before a People's Court, but the two children would be permitted to leave Red China and return to Europe alone.

Somehow or other, this news reached the passengers in the Air France aircraft which was about to take off.

To their great credit, the French diplomats and some German businessmen immediately got off the aircraft and protested. They said firmly that they would not take off unless my wife went with the children, too.

After a long harangue, the Chinese agreed to let my wife put on her clothes and take the children with her. It was certainly a very narrow escape.

* * *

It wasn't until much later—after I had studied Chinese Communism more fully, and discussed it with members of the British Mission—that I realized the Chinese at the airport were acting strictly in accordance with Chairman Mao's teachings.

I recalled from his writings the story of a man seized by the mob, and about to be punished. They decided that they wouldn't inflict punishment immediately; instead, they allowed him to return home. But he wasn't permitted to leave the area, and was told that, at some unexpected moment, he would be re-arrested and severely punished.

For weeks, months, the man lived in perpetual terror, unable to sleep, even sit down; he trembled at the slightest sound, afraid that the mobs were returning to get him.

* * *

My wife and children returned home safely, and a few days after their departure from China the children of the British diplomats were allowed to leave for home. But I was still in China, in Peking and under arrest.

One of the interpreters came up to me. He smiled—as always—and said, "What has happened to you? Have you been abandoned to your fate? Are the friends you helped when they were in trouble now forgetting about you?"

I asked him what he meant.

He smiled again. "We hear from the English Press and radio that a great reception has been accorded to the children of the English diplomats permitted to leave Peking. They have been described as the first British subjects to leave Red China; they've appeared on television, and are feted everywhere. Yet the truth is that your own two children were the first to return home. Why then has nothing been mentioned in the newspapers? Why has the whole matter of the Watt family been completely hushed up? The British public have not been told that you—a British subject—have had your movements restricted and are unable to leave Peking. Why? To my mind, it is all very strange indeed. There must be some sinister reason for it. Why should your Government connive at keeping those facts from the British people?"

They clearly felt that this signified guilt of some kind on my part.

* * *

Left to my own devices in Peking, I now settled into a new routine. Every morning I ordered a taxi, and went round to the office of the British Chargé d'Affaires. They were glad to see me, because they had been put under restriction, which meant that they weren't permitted to leave their area. I read their newspapers which were sent air-mail from Britain.

One morning, in my hotel room, I was listening idly to my short-wave radio, and suddenly picked up an English language broadcast from Peking.

I heard how four British subjects of Chinese origin had entered Red China from the British Crown Colony of Hong Kong. They consisted of a husband and wife and two colleagues who were in China on business. They were seized by the mobs and accused of being "British Imperialist spies".

In the usual manner, they were ordered to make their confessions. Understandably enough, they hadn't realized that anyone accused of a crime had to make confessions in order to receive lenient treatment; nor did they understand that, if they persisted in their innocence, they would be accused of not being honest and would receive very severe punishment.

Those four people persisted in declaiming their innocence. They were, therefore, taken to a trial by the mob, where the prosecutor announced that they had refused to admit guilt and make their confessions, their much sought-after confessions.

To my horror, they were sentenced as follows. The two businessmen received imprisonment for life—which means literally for life. The wife was sentenced to fifteen years in prison. The husband was executed on the spot, there and then.

The broadcast emphasized that the sentences depended very much on the fact that the accused persons had not made confessions.

I cannot stress too strongly the importance of those so-called "confessions" to the warped Communist mind. It must be almost impossible for the democratic people of Britain and the United States to believe the extent to which the Communists of Red China have conspired to degrade human beings.

My initial reaction to the news was that the Chinese Communists were catching too many spies. Instead of being content with trapping one single spy, they were now going all out to discover spies in groups. Surely common sense would tell them that no foreign Power would send in spies in quantity.

Suddenly, I thought about my own position. Perhaps, I reasoned, they'll think that I am a spy.

Now that this spying mania of theirs has been whipped up, the next step will be to turn to me! I had an uneasy feeling that something was brewing and, whatever it was, I certainly wasn't going to enjoy it.

The more I thought about it, the more I began to worry. Finally, I went round to the office of the Chargé d'Affaires.

I said, "Do you think that they could possibly have me on their list as the next victim—as a spy?"

Then, with a lightness which I didn't really feel, I added, "After all, I have taken the odd photograph of wall posters

101

—which most visitors do. But with all this rampage going on, they may well see something sinister in it."

While we were discussing this, a message arrived from my company's manager in Lanchow to tell us that my West German colleague, Peter Deckart, had been arrested by the Lanchow Secret Police. Apparently, my colleagues had just begun breakfast when the police burst in, grabbed Deckart, and led him away to interrogate him in his room. When the others followed to see what was happening, they heard Deckart calling to them through the door, "Those so-and-so's think I'm a spy."

One of the officials said to me, "Perhaps this is it, George. They've been holding you only because they felt that one of your colleagues in Lanchow had been up to something suspicious. Maybe, you're now off the hook?"

I confess that I didn't feel all that confident, as so many spies—or, at least, alleged spies—were being caught at that time.

The position was that West Germany was not represented in Peking diplomatically. There was, however, a West German Press correspondent in Peking, and he was regarded in diplomatic circles as a very unofficial chargé d'affaires; probably even less. It was certainly a most unusual set-up, but in any case, this gentleman was at that time back home in West Germany on holiday.

Of course, the British Mission was powerless to interfere in any way since a West German national had been arrested; but, understandably, they were curious, and, indeed, anxious to discover what was going on. Peter Deckart was after all employed by an Anglo-German company with headquarters in London.

When we finally got through to our colleagues in Lanchow—a long and wearing process by telephone—the conversation was frequently interrupted. It was obvious that the lines were being tapped, and most inexpertly.

We were informed as follows:

"Suddenly, all the interpreters vanished from the hotel. Occasionally, we'd spot one only a few yards away. But, whenever he caught sight of us, he'd run. And when we shouted, 'Hi, there, come back, we want to talk to you, he'd run off even faster."

It was indeed a pathetic situation when an adult man would flee—in obvious terror, too—just because he was about to be asked a question. It was a sobering demonstration of how afraid the Chinese Communists were of committing themselves in conversation with any foreigners—another example of the fear of appearing conspicuous or of accepting responsibility.

The only information we got about Deckart was that he was believed to be in the Friendship Hotel, Lanchow, still. The place was overrun with security forces and the entire top floor declared out of bounds. Barbed wire was ringed round the staircase, and doors built to shut out the top floor. From outside, it could be seen that one of the windows facing the back had recently had iron stanchions added. One assumed, therefore, that Deckart was being held captive in that top-floor room.

He had just been spirited away, and had vanished—as countless foreigners before him had vanished, without trace, in Communist countries.

And so the days continued to pass slowly during September, 1967.

There was, unhappily, no sign of my being let off the hook, as my friends had predicted. I was still under Peking arrest.

Finally, in my fifth week of arrest, I decided to do something positive. I decided to pull Mao's tail. I felt that I had to bring the matter to a head, one way or the other. I asked some members of the British Mission to come to the hotel and have dinner as my guests.

It is important for me to stress here that up to this point —the fifth week after the sacking of the Mission—the diplomats had not been permitted to leave the immediate area of their compound.

They were not allowed to go out socially, although they had been to one or two minor diplomatic meetings, mainly in the afternoon. But they were rigidly barred from going out into the town.

So, forty-eight hours before my dinner party, they applied for formal permission to visit me. To everyone's surprise—especially mine—permission was granted.

I remember the occasion vividly—26 September, 1967. Little did I realize that this would be my last day of freedom, that I would be spirited away and made to vanish from civilized society for nearly three years.

That evening, however, I was in good spirits. Five diplomats arrived—Alastair Hunter with his wife, two young women members of the staff, and another diplomat on a temporary visit to Peking. One of the girls, whose first name was Pat—a jolly, happy-go-lucky, charming person —had been the victim of a most vile assault, at the sacking of the Mission.

Bang on eight o'clock, they arrived as promised; though obviously a bit shaken.

They said that when they left the Mission quarters, just a short distance away, they had been followed by a truck with searchlights playing and sirens blaring.

When they arrived at the hotel, a mob had gathered to spit and sneer at them.

The Chinese, incidentally, don't use handkerchiefs. They feel that it is unsanitary to expel waste matter from the body, parcel it up in cloth, and put it back in their pocket. They spit out all the time—and, speaking from experience, they are certainly most proficient at spitting.

*   *   *

Naturally, as host, I wanted to lay on the very best that money could buy. When I say "money", I mean that I had wads of Chinese Communist yuan. Outside Red China they were absolutely worthless.

I ordered champagne as an apértif—and it was of first-rate French vintage—followed at the meal by Moselle and Claret.

The main dish was Peking duck, a specialty of the house. In Red China, in the midst of universal famine and near-starvation, it is possible to go to a hotel, and eat like a millionaire.

For foreigners and fellow travelers, there was food in

abundance, and of very good quality. I had first observed this in Lanchow, where it was impossible to buy eggs in the local market, while we could have three or four eggs each for breakfast.

The Chinese love to put on a ritzy show for foreigners —especially for those believed to have Maoist sympathies.

So, although we sat down eagerly to a magnificent spread, we harbored no illusions. We felt sorry—and I say this most sincerely—because we knew that most of those who served our meal had probably never tasted duck in their lives.

The party went with a swing. The diplomats relaxed. The champagne gave out, and I ordered more. The girls were enjoying themselves. I began to feel in good form. I can still see young Pat laughing. Horrible memories were being erased. When we asked her how she felt when she'd been dragged off by the Red Guards, she replied, "All I wanted was just to go to the 'loo'."

I remember looking round that evening at my guests, and when I saw them so obviously happy, I felt really proud to be British.

Later, in my prison cell, in low spirits, I would often think of that evening. I was cheered in retrospect by the sight of Pat's happy face, and I have often thought that, if I had the time all over again, I wouldn't change one detail. It was a most rewarding dinner party; a highlight of my life.

When the party ended I went to see them to their car, mainly because I had spotted a crowd of people gathered —ready to spit.

As we came down the stairs, we saw two security officers standing by the reception desk, with their elbows on the counter. They must have been standing there for some time, as we could see a clear semi-circle of spittle on the floor.

They straightened up as if for some kind of action, but we pushed past. Some of the hotel staff and bystanders stood by, hissing and catcalling. But I quickly got my guests into the car. Immediately, the lights of the truck parked behind them blazed, and sirens wailed. Out of the darkness, scores of people emerged from all directions to converge on the car. My guests managed to make a clean getaway, and I ran quickly back into the hotel.

I knew that Alastair Hunter had risked his car just to come to my dinner. Some of the other members of the diplomatic staff had had their cars burned out on the day of the attack. As the future was so uncertain, he had taken the precaution of selling his car to an Eastern European embassy. It is well known that Eastern European embassies are top-heavy with "diplomats" of the strong-arm variety, but have a shortage of motor vehicles.

When I first went to the Soviet Union in 1966, I inevitably noticed that there were more cars every night outside my local public house in the West of England than there were in Moscow's Red Square.

*　　*　　*

Going upstairs to my room, I passed a little bar on the first floor. The barman held out a glass of beer, although I hadn't ordered it. I took it. As I stood there drinking, a member of the hotel staff arrived with one of my shirts freshly washed and ironed from the hotel laundry. I had never had laundry delivered at such at late hour, but I told him to put it on my bill, as usual. Then came a surprise. He insisted on cash.

Suddenly, I didn't feel so full of well-being. I sensed that the "Big Grab" was due at any moment. Then one of the hotel office staff arrived holding some bill forms. They were making up my account. The bill for the dinner that evening was on top.

I walked up to my room and picked up the telephone to tell the British Mission that I was about to be nabbed.

Before I could ask for the number, the door burst open and half a dozen Red Guards piled in. They grabbed my arms, twisting them up behind my back. A gun was rammed into my side, and one of them wrapped his arm around my neck.

I was told, "Don't make a noise." I could hardly breathe.

I was marched off to a large room on the same floor

which was often used as a reception or meeting hall. It was crowded. Among the throng were some of the waiters who had served that magnificent dinner. They still wore their white coats. There wasn't a sound as I was brought in.

Behind a table in the middle of the room sat six men in grey uniforms.

I was placed on a chair in front of the table, and for ten minutes nothing was said. Everybody just stood and stared rigidly, pointing at me with stabbing fingers. . . .

Mao Tse-tung has a saying: A thousand pointing fingers, and a man dies without a sickness.

Then I saw Shah standing in front of the crowd. He said to me: "You know why you have been brought here. You must understand that you do not have diplomatic immunity."

I had enough champagne and brandy inside me to give me Dutch courage.

I said, "From what I have seen, it isn't worth having. Perhaps I'm better without it."

Mr. Shah said, "You are being insolent. Be careful. . . . You are now before the People's Court."

I had not been properly arrested. No formal charges had been read out. I had no lawyer. Yet, quite clearly, I was the defendant at a trial.

I resolved to keep a check on my tongue. Clever stuff would get me nowhere.

Shah took fifteen minutes to read the list of crimes I was alleged to have committed. They said that my wife had committed great crimes—*great* crimes—in Communist China everything is *great;* nothing happens at ordinary level.

I had given aid to the British diplomats when they were "receiving punishment". I had performed deliberate acts of provocation—one of which was to buy wickerwork baskets for one of the wives from a Peking department store.

I had spread false rumors connected with the delay of my family's departure, "thus trying to drive a wedge between the Chinese people and their foreign friends".

My final insult to the Chinese people was that I had

"publicly entertained the Imperialist British diplomats while they were under restriction".

BUT AT THIS STAGE THERE WAS NO MENTION OF ANY ACCUSATION THAT I WAS A SPY.

* * *

Mr. Shah took my wallet out from my pocket. He counted out some notes, kept them (this was the price of the air fare) and handed me an air ticket. . . . "This is your aircraft reservation. You are under arrest, and the Peking Revolutionary Committee has decided to return you to Lanchow where, it is understood, new charges are pending.

"It is not necessary for you to make a plea at this time. But we advise you to admit your crimes in full. The Chinese people may show you some leniency."

I said nothing. I was taken back to my hotel room, and locked in with three guards armed with rifles.

They indicated that I should pack my bags. I did so. I poured myself a beer, lay on the bed, and dozed off.

I was roused by one of the guards poking me in the stomach with his rifle. It was 4 a.m. I had been asleep for two or three hours.

When I reached the airport it was dawn—a beautiful dawn, with a warm glow.

CHAPTER XI

Return to Lanchow

I shall never forget that morning . . . 27 September, 1967. I had been in China for nine months. If all had gone well the plant on which I had been working for Vickers-Zimmer should now have been nearly finished. I should have been preparing for the journey back to Britain. Instead, I was wondering whether I should ever see my family or my country again.

An imposing reception had been arranged for my return to Lanchow.

As soon as I stepped out of the aircraft I was surrounded by about 30 security police armed with rifles. They formed a box of six lines of five men. I was in the middle.

Thousands of jeering, chanting Chinese lined the railings by the reception buildings. We started marching towards them, and I knew that I was to be put on show.

A few feet from the railings we turned and twice marched up and down the full length of the crowd. Then I was taken into the reception lounge.

Fifteen minutes later, one of the senior escorts who had been with me on the aircraft marched in carrying a large document.

He spoke to me for the first time since leaving Peking. . . .

"Attention, Watt. Stand here." And then he began reading from the document:

"George Watt, a British Imperialist spy, has been detected by the masses. . . ."

His word droned on. But one word kept hammering through my brain—SPY.

What could I say in response to this nonsensical charge?

I had planned to make a guarded reply to that ridiculous list of so-called crimes which had been listed in Peking, in the hope that the Chinese would live up to their promise of clemency.

But how could I confess to being a spy? It might mean risking being shot for something that I had not done.

I tried to concentrate on what the man was saying. . . .

"During your stay in Lanchow, you stole a large amount of important intelligence about Chinese military and economic and political affairs. In addition, you took photographs of prohibited areas. . . ." And this was followed by the list of "crimes" from Peking.

I was told that I would be held at the Friendship Hotel under armed guard while being investigated by the Public Security Bureau.

I was placed in a room which had been converted into

a temporary cell. Wooden slats three inches wide had been screwed across the windows, just six inches apart. Two armed guards were with me in that room during the whole period I was there.

The investigation of the charges against me lasted for six months.

I was interrogated almost daily—sometimes three times a day. The questioning would start at 9 a.m., and carry on till five o'clock. The interrogators would then give me an hour's break, and start again. The evening sessions usually lasted until 11 p.m. Sometimes they went on into the early hours of the morning. Occasionally, after being dismissed at night, I would be awakened at one, two, or even three o'clock in the morning, to face more questioning.

For all my interrogations I was taken from my room to another just across the corridor. I was told to sit on a wooden chair in a corner. That chair was a torture instrument in itself.

The seat, a natural width at the front, converged until the rear edge was no more than three inches wide. The back, too, was only three inches wide, and set absolutely straight up and down.

I couldn't lean back in comfort, and the hard, sharp edges cut into my flesh. If I leaned forward and rested my elbows on my knees, I would be told not to be disrespectful to the court, and to sit up straight.

As the days passed, I grew more and more weary—so tired that at times I would doze. Sometimes a guard would jerk me awake with the tip of his bayonet. Not a savage jab, but enough to rip my shirt and nick my skin.

At the end of that six months, my chest and stomach were marked by 50 or 60 such nicks.

At all times a bright light shone directly in my face. I had two main inquisitors, whom I privately named Mr. Rage and Mr. Kind.

Mr. Rage would rant and threaten me with dire consequences unless I confessed. When I refused, he would apparently lose his temper and shriek: "Dirty British spy! Why waste time with him? Let us take him out and shoot him now."

Mr. Kind would intercede, saying, "Yes, I know he deserves it. But he has a wife and two lovely children. It would be terrible to think that they would never see him again because he has been used by the British Imperialists. Let us give him a chance to confess his crimes."

They would appear to be arguing this out among themselves. But always there was an interpreter there to translate every word for my benefit.

I began to hate Mr. Rage, and to think that I would have no hope at all had it not been for the intervention of Mr. Kind.

They had me in a daze, day and night. They went through my family history, demanding the names and ages of every relative on both sides of my family.

Then they would snap out threats, such as: "Now we shall break you down, expose your false family, and find out who you *really* are."

"Where did you do your military training? Where did you receive your espionage training?"

They seized on the fact that I had once been with an American construction company, and converted that simple fact into a link with the American C.I.A.

My normal weight is 14 stone. By the end of that six months, I reckon I was down to 11.

The same questions were repeated over and over again. I felt I'd have gone mad if it had not been for the apparent thoughtfulness of Mr. Kind. Several times I fell out of my chair in a state of near collapse. Then they would drag me off to my room, dump me on the bed, and let rest. But only for 20 minutes. Then they would lug me back into the interrogation room.

At one point, I asked them why they spirited Anthony Grey away, why was he under arrest. One doesn't normally expect a reply to questions immediately; but, next day, one of the interpreters said: "Mr. Grey is a reporter from Reuter, whose head office is in London. During the time that the Chinese were making, shall we say, rather forceful demonstrations, Mr. Grey decided to leave his home and move in with none other than the British Chargé d'Affaires, Sir Donald Hopson. Because of this, the Chinese Commu-

111

nists felt that Mr. Grey did not wish to appear to be neutral; he had allied himself with the British diplomats . . . who in our opinion were under *criticism*. Therefore how can you recognize this man as an international reporter with an international news agency. He is a British subject from London—so that is why he was removed from the scene."

He then added: "You yourself, George Watt, were also passing through Peking, on your way to Hong Kong with your wife and children. But you chose to ally yourself with the British diplomats who were under criticism—a deliberate act of provocation to the Chinese people. So now you are in a predicament, and are also under criticism."

One day when I was being questioned, a Chinese interrogator lunged at me with his knife, and pushed it through the back of my hand. I carry the scar to this day.

He smiled, and said smugly, "Very, very sorry."

Trying not to be too upset, I wrapped the wound with my handkerchief; blood spurted out all down my trousers.

It wasn't so much the injury that infuriated me. It was painful, of course. But what had me confused was that someone should deliberately stab me, and then say hypocritically, "Very, very sorry." There was a frightening, abnormal aspect of it—almost uncanny. It tended to upset my entire line of reasoning.

They carried out this war of nerves when I was in bed. Just when I had dropped off to sleep, a group would come in, shake me awake. When I sat up, startled, and blinking in the light they had switched on and directed into my eyes, they would murmur, "Very, very sorry."

To say the least, it was unnerving.

Then they would say, solicitously, "Very, sorry, have you been sleeping? Sorry, but we would like to ask you some questions."

This abject apology, coupled with a deliberate act to cause me discomfort, even pain, soon drove me from a rational line of reasoning.

On Christmas Day, 1967, I was sitting alone in my room, waiting for the interpreters to arrive—the only respite I knew I was likely to have to relieve the tedium.

My mind went back to a year earlier to the dinner we had with the little piglets that had died.

I was re-living those incidents—all I had to occupy my time—when the door was unlocked. I looked up to greet the interpreters for their usual session of interrogation. But there was one important difference in their appearance. This time, they were smiling—indeed, beaming. I knew, however, from bitter experience, that when they smiled there was something in store for me—and not necessarily pleasant.

This group was led by Mr. Lou, a smooth gentleman I'd grown to distrust, and even hate. He wore a perpetual smile like an Oriental from an early Hollywood film. His upper teeth protruded obscenely, and had the appearance of a rabbit in the last throes of myxomatosis.

Lou intoned sententiously, "We understand that today is Christmas Day, a Christian holiday. On this day, as a kindness, we intend to let you participate in the meal served to your comrades in the lower floor of this hotel."

To my surprise, he handed me a menu, and with a smile said, "Please select from this what you would like to eat for your Christmas dinner."

I was overwhelmed with gratitude, and even felt a little ashamed that I had, perhaps, misjudged Mr. Lou. I decided that I had become a little too hard and unrelenting. These people weren't really so devious, after all.

Anyway, I determined not to pass up this opportunity of enjoying a good meal.

Hungrily, greedily, I looked through the menu, hoping that I wasn't dwelling too long on the items—savoring each course vicariously. Finally, I chose duck. Dutifully, Lou wrote down my order, and left the room. I remember feeling completely bemused.

That evening I was sitting at the table, facing the wall, with a few Chinese propaganda books in front of me, when a group arrived.

The two soldiers who guarded me night and day moved to one side. They lowered their fixed bayonets.

A steward, grinning mischievously, placed a large silver plattee on my table, surrounded by a domed cover. I touched it gingerly with a finger. It was oven-hot. The steward, with elaborate ceremony, handed me a napkin.

They were all watching me closely. Carefully, in silence, I lifted the cover, to disclose a plate. And on the plate was—one bare bone.

This was the Chinese Communists' idea of a joke. On Christmas Day.

Everyone started to laugh. I'm afraid I failed to react to their sense of humor. I could only glare back, dumbfounded. Privately, I thought how childish they were.

Lou, the interpreter, was doubled up with laughter at my expense. As I stared back at him, with what I hoped was an inscrutable face, I suddenly remembered. . . .

When I first arrived in Lanchow, Lou was the chief of a group of interpreters attached to a British construction company, Simon Carves.

This was normal procedure; every company had accredited interpreters. But Lou was different. I had regarded him as almost an imbecile. He couldn't coordinate his movements. One would find him in the evening, lying around in the entrance to the hotel, or sprawled half asleep behind the counter of the hotel shop, among the fruit and vegetables and soft drinks. He looked like a leftover from an early Hollywood Western film, the kind of character played by Walter Brennan. Lou, obviously, had a "screw loose" somewhere. Indeed, some of the engineers' wives arranged for him to take the children out for walks, with the idea that this would keep him out of mischief.

But he was always to be seen hanging around the quarters. Most of us felt sorry for him, I think, although, he did speak fairly good English.

Imagine my surprise one day when—a few days before Christmas—a stranger walked into the interrogation room. He was obviously a Chinese Army officer of high rank. He was smart, erect, well groomed, commanding in appearance and voice. He was greeted with punctilious salutes and subservient bows and handshakes. With enormous self-composure, he acknowledged their salaams, and sat down at the head of the table. Who could this God-like figure be?

114

I looked on in amazement. The stranger was none other than Mr. Lou. What a transformation. Gone was the half-witted, straw-in-mouth Tom Sawyer dossing down in the barn. This character was as if fresh out of Sandhurst—a budding general.

What a magnificent act, just for the benefit of the visiting Europeans. But why? Why?

* * *

Anyway, the Christmas period passed, and I got to know Lou rather better.

My makeshift prison in the hotel had bars across the windows which were obscured by brown paper, pasted on the inside.

Sometimes, between long periods of interrogation, I would lean against the windows; and, when I thought the guards weren't peering through the spy-hole at me, I'd make a little tear in the paper with my fingernail.

When I looked out I noticed my colleagues playing football in the courtyard at the back. I knew then that they were not carrying on with their everyday work. And I knew, from the screams I could occasionally hear when they were being interrogated, that there was still a lot of heavy fighting going on. How I longed to join my friends, if only to get some exercise.

I only dared look for a few seconds at a time, as I knew I was under constant observation. Suddenly, however, I saw not only colleagues from my own company, the Lurgi Company, and Simon Carves, but the familiar figure of Mr. Lou. There he was, playing football. But his movements were again all disjointed. When the ball flew past the makeshift goal posts of piled coats, Lou would run after it in his loping style, pick up the ball, and try to kick it back to the players. More often than not, the ball would bounce, he'd mis-kick it, and fall down, and everyone would laugh at his antics.

I watched him running around, rolling about; and, then, when the match was finished, he insisted on carrying the ball back to the dressing rooms.

Minutes later, he'd stride into the interrogation room, smart in his uniform, looking really "with it". A completely different person.

And that is the point I want to stress, especially for future visitors to Red China. The very friendly interpreter who pretends to be your long-lost brother may well be a member of the Secret Police.

*   *   *

One night they took me upstairs to the flat roof of the hotel. I confess I was bewildered and not a little frightened. They stood me against a wall—actually the wall of a billiard room. My back was to the glass french windows. Six soldiers lined up in front, pointing rifles at me.

The Chinese officer in charge of them shouted out a command. I couldn't understand what he said, but the tone was eloquent enough. I thought to myself, "This is it."

But nothing happened. I was terrified. The sweat streamed down my face. The silence, the utter inaction was unnerving. . . .

The soldiers moved over, pushed me away, so that I was standing against a thick brick wall. The thought crossed my mind that they were more concerned about the glass than about me.

My heart was beating loudly. I felt so short of breath. Then I decided to be resigned. Any moment now I'd know the answer. But, please God, let it be over soon.

Ridiculously, I thought of my old Irish grandmother, long since departed. She used to regale me with her religious theories. Her reckoning was, "If you're a good little boy, you'll go to Heaven." Her interpretation of Heaven was that I'd flutter around with a pair of wings. If, however, I was a bad little boy, I'd be down in Hell, where I'd spend most of my time shovelling coal on a great fire.

As I stood there—the Chinese soldiers levelling their rifles—I tried to get what cheer I could from the position. At least, I thought, any moment now I'm going to know if there was any substance in my grandmother's philosophy.

So there I stood. There was no use trying to make a

116

break for it. I just prayed that it would all end quickly and as painlessly as possible.

Again the officer in charge barked out a command. The rifles clicked.

My mind felt numbed. Was I shot? Should I fall down? Was I only in a state of shock? But I felt my legs giving way—would I fall?

The officer strode over to me, and said slowly and distinctly, "We shall give you another chance. You can now go back to your room."

I felt stunned. For a moment or two I remember wondering if I was dreaming the whole thing. I took a step forward and almost fell. Two hefty soldiers grabbed me by the arms and half-walked, half-frog-marched, me back to my makeshift cell.

They slumped me into my chair, and the leader said, "Now you can continue your confessions."

They put a pen into my hand. But when I tried to write I only succeeded in making an unintelligible scrawl. I was trembling violently and was suffering badly from shock. I pulled myself together and tried again. This time I pushed the the pen right through the few pages into the desk, and snapped off the nib.

The guard looked at me with a mixture of scorn and pity, and said stiffly, "We shall continue later," and left the room.

* * *

And so the interrogations continued. But during this time I noticed that the interrogators were bringing up a third portion of food.

Up until then there had been portions for only two prisoners. I knew that my West German colleague, Peter Deckart, was being held somewhere else in the hotel, probably in the other wing alongside me on the top floor.

Then I noticed that a room quite close to me had guards posted outside. As this had happened only a few days previously I assumed—rightly, as it turned out—that the Chinese Secret Police had arrested a third person.

117

I was most curious to discover who this was, but did not have to wait long for the answer. During my next interrogation I was asked about a German employed by the Lurgi company—Kurtz von Xylander.

He was proud of the title "von", and was the son of the late Lieutenant-General Xylander, one of Hitler's foremost military leaders in Europe during the Second World War.

I thought it interesting, too, that when I looked through my little paper slit in the window, I never saw Xylander. Yet I knew him to be a most active type, fond of exercise, and indeed of all sports.

So, I thought, the third prisoner on the top floor is without doubt Kurtz von Xylander.

I realized that the Lanchow Secret Police were now following the example of the Peking Secret Police. They were no longer content with catching suspected spies; they now wanted to capture groups of spies. A little too ambitious—surely, I thought, there must be people in authority in Peking who can understand how illogical and ridiculous this is. But the Chinese didn't seem to see it like that, and it looked as if the Secret Police in the various cities were competing with each other to see how many foreigners could be arrested.

CHAPTER XII

I Confess

I finally decided, when they produced photographs of mine which were allegedly of prohibited areas, that I would have to make some sort of "confession". The pictures were nothing more than snapshots of the Yellow River and of anti-British posters stuck up outside the hotel for all to see.

I recalled some excellent advice I had received at the British Mission. A senior British diplomat had taken me aside, and said: "Look, George, you are not being held here for nothing. You are being held so that they can discredit you—and the British. You can be sure of one thing—because by now you have more than an inkling of how their minds work—this situation will not end with the Chinese making apologies. It will end with the Chinese accusing you of something very serious. When they do this, the best way out is to make some sort of token admission. Don't dare tell them that they could possibly have made a mistake, because they will then insist that you are not being truthful, and that your attitude is going from bad to worse. . . . Say, instead, something on the lines of *I'm very sorry for breaking your beautiful laws*."

I repeated this to the diplomat . . . "O.K., I'll say to them, I'm very sorry for breaking your beautiful laws."

And he broke in hurriedly, clearly alarmed; "Good Heavens, don't use the word *beautiful*. I was only being sarcastic. One thing the Chinese cannot stand is anyone trying to take the Mickey out of them, or even jest. Be very solemn, very apologetic. Then admit to more or less whatever they dream up that you have committed."

This was the official British advice.

I knew then that if I didn't do something to satisfy those madmen, they would have me in and out of that room for the rest of my life.

Very guardedly I said, "I wouldn't exactly say that I am a spy. But—*from your point of view*—I know I am a spy. I am prepared to admit this, if you can differentiate between a trained spy and one who is an engineer, and not a trained agent."

The answer was: "We cannot differentiate. You are either a spy or you are not. So admit you are."

This line of conversation went on for days. Then Mr. Kind, who for all those months had been the nearest thing to a friend I was likely to find, suddenly exploded.

"This," he roared, "is the end. I have done all I can for you. I have been your friend, and you have betrayed that friendship. Now I am in trouble. This is your last possible chance. There is your confession. Sign it now, or pay the price of your guilt."

He threw about 50 typed pages into my lap.

I didn't even try to read them. One of the guards turned the pages for me. I signed each one. As I wrote, the signatures looked too large, sweeping up and down too far in both directions, and sprawling almost across the entire page.

Then I was allowed to sleep.

I awoke next day at 10 a.m. It was 14 March, 1968. The events of the day before were like a nightmare recalled, but I knew it was no dream. I was bitter and disappointed that they had managed to defeat me—however temporarily.

But I had no time to sit and brood. About ten guards marched in, pushed me to the floor, and then thrust me down again as I struggled to my knees. Then they dragged me out along the corridor, and pushed and pulled as I bumped on my side down the stairs of the Friendship Hotel.

I was dumped into a jeep and, accompanied by guards and two interpreters, was driven off to Anti-Revisionist Square where, months before, I had seen Chinese hung and tortured for their alleged crimes. The "masses" were today again assembled in their thousands.

The guards took me through a side door of the Anti-Revisionist Hall, on the edge of the square, and marched me into a massive auditorium. Then they placed me on a platform.

The hall was crammed with shouting Chinese. As I was marched through those ranks of hate, they shook fists at me, and spat . . . most of them with uncomfortably good aim.

On the platform I was put facing a huge picture of Mao-Tse-tung, edged on each side by heavy red drapes. I remember thinking ironically, "That's about the friendliest looking face in the whole hall."

An interpreter just below my platform was telling me: *Bow your head, George Watt. . . . Bow to the masses.*

A young woman judge read out the charges, then read out my confession. It took about an hour. I didn't really listen.

All this was being relayed by loudspeaker to that huge, writhing mob in the square.

I heard the interpreter calling to me: "Come. Come down, George Watt. The masses are calling you."

I was marched back through the hall to the front entrance, through to the doors, and out on to a big terrace built about 10ft above the level of the square. The only means of approach were by stairs at each side, guarded by armed troops.

There were also armed troops on the terrace, where I was forced to stand with bowed head, while the mob howled and tried to spit up at me.

All the time, the soldiers prodded me with their rifle muzzles, to move me from one side of the terrace to the other, so that I was displayed to the best advantage. Within seconds, my ribs were aching and my body stiff from those prods; yet still they came. No matter where I moved, there was no escape.

Sweat poured down my face, and I felt myself sinking. Then I was on the ground, and the sky was swimming around—filled with watching Chinese faces.

They carried me back into the hall, and sat me in a chair for a few minutes. Then I heard the interpreter saying: "The masses are calling you again. Can't you hear them? You must go and bow to them, to show your repentance."

Once again I was marched out. My knees were wobbly, and I wanted to be sick. Again those rifle muzzles began prodding, and went on prodding until I collapsed again.

Once more I was taken back into the hall, and allowed to recover slightly before being marched out again.

I don't remember how many times this happened, but I have a feeling that I had to take eight or nine of those horrific curtain calls. Again I collapsed. When I finally came to in the hall, I had the impression that I had been out for a long time.

My right eye was closed, and the blood from a rip in my left ear was pouring down the inside of the neck of my shirt. Indeed, I could feel it streaming down to my waistline.

My eye and ear have been permanently damaged by that battering. My vision is blurred, and my hearing impaired.

Dimly, I heard the interpreter's voice again. It seemed to be coming from a long way off. Gradually, I realized that he was giving me different orders this time.

121

"Run. Run. You have to run, George Watt. Quickly, before it is too late."

Fuddled and bemused, I struggled to my feet. Then the soldiers gathered round, and half carrying me, got me to the side door by which we had entered this torture chamber. I was dumped into the back of the jeep. Lying there, I could just see over the tailboard.

People were running towards us. They began to chase us, waving and shouting. Some had broken down the doors of Anti-Revisionist Hall, and had poured through the hall in a bid to get at me.

As we left the hall after the trial, the masses tried to cut off my escape. The impression I got was that they were attempting to surround the jeep. The scene was like a human sea. Thousands, tens of thousands upon tens of thousands of people were massed together, swaying, shouting, and screaming as they advanced over the mud walls towards the Anti-Revisionist Hall.

I remember thinking that day that if I had had a machine gun with an endless supply of bullets, it would have been virtually impossible to have stopped them. They represented such a solid phalanx, heedless of personal danger, that they could never be stopped by conventional weapons. Certainly not people who had been trained to practice the military tactics of a "human sea".

That incident remains vividly in my mind. It is linked with another experience when I visited a Chinese nursery school for toddlers being trained in the art of bayonet-fighting.

The jeep driver speeded up, cutting across a piece of waste land as a short cut to the road. The vehicle bounced high and hard over boulders and holes, but still that crowd came on. By now the main mob from the square was racing across to try to head off the jeep from the road.

We made the road with only yards to spare. I stared, almost hypnotized, at the frantic mob as we sped away.

I was taken to Lanchow jail. They put me into a cell. But all I knew about it was that the bench on which I was lying felt like a bed of stones.

Pulling open my shirt, I looked at my body. It was

covered with hundreds of little bruises . . . the pattern left by the rifle muzzles. In some places, there were so many joined together that it looked like chain mail.

Then I heard a voice saying in English, "Here is some water. Drink it. It is all over."

I gulped most of the water. With the remainder, I bathed my eye which felt as big as a golf ball.

I lay there. It seemed—the first time for years—that everything was quiet. . . .

* * *

As I lay there on the wooden plank bed in a daze I could hear the roar of the angry crowd.

The noise grew louder, and I guessed that the mob were through the main gates of the prison and in the outer courtyard.

Above the turmoil, I heard someone yell, "Yingo"—the Chinese word for "English".

An interpreter came in. "There is trouble outside", he said. "The people think you have been let off too lightly. They want you to hang."

But there was nothing I could do. I just lay there, as calmly as I could, waiting for whatever was to come.

Suddenly there was a tremendous burst of cheering, and I guessed that the crowd had broken through into the inner courtyard. There was now only one set of gates between them and me.

The pandemonium last for no more than 20 minutes or so but it seemed long enough.

Then the row began to fade, until there was complete silence.

The interpreter reappeared. This time, he was smiling.

"Do not worry any more," he said. "It is all over. The masses were demanding your execution. But there was a wicked landowner in the prison who had been here for some time. He had refused to repent and remold himself. The masses have now taken him, and he will be punished in your place."

I felt sick.

He spoke as if the handing over of a human being to a blood-crazed mob was an everyday occurrence. Could it be true? Or was his story all part of a systematic torture? Had the whole performance been staged to terrorize me?

There was no way of knowing. I don't suppose there ever will be.

I was kept in Lanchow jail for four days. I was in constant agony from the beating I'd received at my "trial". My right eye was still closed, and the throbbing seemed to knock the very brains in my skull. The rip in my left ear was still oozing blood. And as I turned and twisted in half-sleep, half-nightmare, the wound kept opening.

Not once was I offered medical attention. And I was determined not to beg for anything. I decided I'd rather rot first.

CHAPTER XIII

The Ideological Remolding Prison

On 18 March, 1968—the day after St. Patrick's Day—I was flown back to Peking.

I couldn't help laughing on the flight, although I did try to pretend I'd been seized by a fit of coughing, when one of the officials on board banged his head on the luggage rack when he stood up to read *The Thoughts of Mao*.

I had been escorted on board the little Russian Aleutian aircraft by half a dozen security guards armed with rifles. As they chained me to my seat I couldn't help wondering where they thought I'd escape to. It was typical of the stupid, blundering way the Chinese have of overdoing everything; six "gorillas" just to guard one Irishman!

I noticed that the stewardess had a copy of a local newspaper, and was obviously reading out my name and description to the passengers. "George Watt, of Vickers-Zimmer", I heard her say, and the Chinese turned round and stared at me like something in a zoo. Then they shook their fists at me, booed, and screamed abuse. I couldn't make out details of what they were saying, but clearly they weren't singing my praises.

A fascinating aspect of this scene for me was that no matter how hard I tried, not one of them would catch my eye. I looked around slowly at every face—about twenty in all—and not one had the courage to meet even this mild challenge. They would look above my head, to one side or the other, but no one would comfort me as I sat there heavily guarded and in chains. For me, once again, it indicated the spineless, shifty nature of the Communist Chinese.

When we arrived in Peking a security car drove on to the tarmac, right up to the aircraft. Some of the passengers took this chance to complain to my guards about the indignity of having to travel in the company of a chained criminal.

In the car I lay on the floor, while they sat in the back seat with their feet on top of me, and kept stamping up and down.

The car didn't take me straight to the Ideological Prison but to Peking Prison, where I was to be held overnight.

I was taken into a small room, where about two dozen people sat staring at me. Here again, I thought, another case of the many trying to do the work of the few. I could judge from the noise of the mob outside that I'd be expected to put on some kind of entertainment for them.

I thought that I might escape lightly—being spat at several hundred times. That, however, was not to be. The mob was determined that they were going to see the victim in some considerable pain.

They grabbed hold of me, and twisted my left arm up my back. I was pulled and frog-marched round the yard several times. I kept stumbling. My whole back and neck was a mass of pain, and I knew that my shoulder was dislocated.

I faintly remember running down a corridor, with cell doors flashing past, until I was stopped at a door, and thrown bodily into the darkness. I crashed up against the opposite wall which was only about 6ft inside the door.

I lay there until I had gathered my wits together. I

125

don't know how long it was. There was no furniture in the cell; it was completely bare, 6 ft. by 6 ft.

I knew that the first thing was to try to get my arm back into position. I got my right arm round behind me, and tugged at my little finger. The pain was excruciating, and I think I must have fainted.

Anyway, I did get my arm back in position, because, when I woke again—some hours later—I was lying on the cold stone floor. People were looking in at me, and I was covered in spittle. They must have been spitting on me as I lay there unconscious.

I had spent the night half-asleep and half-conscious. I was roused at first light, but not allowed to wash. My face was filthy, bruised, and streaked with dried blood. My right eye was still closed; my jacket was in tatters, and my shirt torn and bloodstained.

The cell door opened and I was marched out into the yard and bundled into a truck. I was handcuffed and my legs were chained together. Six guards with rifles clambered into the back of the truck with me, and in this manner I was driven to the so-called Ideological Remoulding Prison.

When the truck stopped, I was allowed to sit up, but all I could see was a massive wrought iron gate. I could hear chains grating as the gate was wound up, and we passed slowly beneath it.

We stopped at another large gate set in a high wall. The gate opened and we drove on into a courtyard, to stop in front of yet another gate. It too swung wide, and I was in the main yard of the Peking "Ideological Remoulding Center". This, I knew, was an establishment which deals with foreigners reluctant to acknowledge the superiority of all things Chinese Communist.

On the high walls were lines of wires, which I supposed were electrified. On each corner was a machine-gun post.

I was pushed into Cell No. 5 on the ground floor. It was about 15 ft. by 10 ft. and about 10 ft. high. The furniture consisted of one chair, one small table, a bed of four wooden planks without mattress, and a pail. There were no blankets or coverings of any kind on the bed. On a wall was the ubiquitous picture of Mao Tse-tung. Above it were two tiny barred windows, thick with the grime of years.

I dug my nail into the "bed", and noticed that it was of soft wood. I tried to cheer myself up by reflecting that this is what the Chinese would call "another little kindness". Not that it would make much difference when I was sleeping on it.

The door opened, and I was served my first breakfast, a "normal three-course breakfast". I was offered some sludge from a dirty bucket of "rice gritty". (I made the private reservation—however vulgar—that "grit" was not the correct designation.)

The three courses were as follows: if I dug the ladle deep into the bucket I could retrieve a mixture of rice, dirt, and stones. Halfway up, I could get a few flakes of rice, mixed with liquid starch. If, however, I preferred a light breakfast all I had to do was insert the ladle in the top layer of the muck. Hey presto! Liquid starch only.

Mind you, it took me some days of trial and error to distinguish between the three courses of this gourmet's delight.

Before long I was marched off to the office of a man who spoke English, and who was introduced as my tutor in Maoism. For many months to come he was to be virtually the only person I would speak to, for it was made clear to me that I should not, under any circumstances, attempt to communicate with fellow prisoners. My sentence was to carry an inhumane ruling—solitary confinement, except for the words spoken to me by the Chinese authorities or, in other words, my tutor.

For me, this was a cruel, soul-destroying punishment; but the Chinese had their reasons for imposing this ruling. In the first place, they didn't want the identities of other prisoners to be disclosed—they didn't want prisoners due for early release to return to the free world and reveal the names of those still held in custody. But there was another reason, too: any social contact with other prisoners would upset the plans of the Communists to "condition" minds. I cannot stress too firmly that imprisonment in Red China is not merely a matter of confining a man behind bars.

The Chinese feel that they have the right to use force, and to brainwash a prisoner with Communist ideology.

The first thing my tutor did was to give me four paperback volumes in English. They were, of course, *The Selected Works of Mao Tse-tung* and *The Thoughts of Mao.* He told me what a valuable gift they were and asked me to turn to page 137 and read out what the Chairman had written.

I had read it aloud. Part of it ran: *We should not insult them [prisoners], take away their personal effects, or try to exact recantations from them; but, without exception, should treat them sincerely and kindly.*

"You see," said the tutor, "it is up to you to help yourself by becoming ideologically remolded. You must study these books; if you choose the correct path you will find the people lenient."

It was more than clear that their plan was to brainwash me, but the one thought that kept drumming through my mind was: *"I've got to beat them, I've got to beat them."*

Back in my cell, the tutor pointed to Mao's picture and said: "The Chairman has put rice in the bowls of the people. You are still alive—thanks to his teachings." Still pointing to the picture, he added: "Before each meal you must show your gratitude. Bow to the Chairman, and say *Wan Sui.*"

This phrase (pronounced "One Swee") means "Ten thousand years of life". The Chinese are constantly wishing this to Mao.

I had no intention of wishing Mao *Wan Sui,* and when lunch arrived—a soggy mess of rice dotted with potatoes and carrots which had been neither peeled nor washed—I completely ignored Mao.

The guards must have been watching me through the observation peep-hole in the door, for the tutor paid a special visit to tell me: "Your attitude is wrong, and will do you no good. You must always remember that Chairman Mao is YOUR leader."

I did not relish the thought of bowing to Mao. On the other hand, I wanted to stay out of trouble—and alive.

It happened that I was sorting through a few belongings

I had been allowed to keep—some blank diaries, a ball-point pen, one or two items of underwear, some hanker-chiefs. Tucked away in one of the diaries was a fourpenny British stamp.

I looked at the image of the Queen on the stamp. To me, in that cell, 6,000 miles away from Britain and civilization, it provided a tangible symbol of a way of life which people in Britain take for granted.

Waiting until I was fairly certain that I was not being watched I opened the drawer in the table under Mao's picture. On the interior of one side I found a small wooden strut which swivelled easily on one small tack. I slipped the stamp behind the strut, and at dinner time—the food was no different from lunch—I put my plan into action.

Leaving the drawer open just wide enough, I placed the bowl of filthy goo on the table. Then, stretching out one hand, as if resting lightly on the table, I carefully swivelled the strut until the stamp was in view.

Then—and only then—did I bow. I didn't look at Mao. Instead, I kept my eyes on the Queen's image, and wished her *Wan Sui*.

It fooled the guards that day, and every day. From the peep-hole only my bowed back could be seen.

For nearly two years and six months, that stamp was my anchor. I still have it and shall always keep it.

*   *   *

During those first months in the Ideological Remolding Center I was highly curious about my fellow prisoners. There were obviously several non-Asians in nearby cells. They were mainly Americans and I think there was one Englishman there—a fair-haired man of whom I caught a glimpse only once. I never saw him again, nor heard him speak—his cell was too far down the corridor.

I am pretty sure that there was a woman in the cell next to mine. I heard her coughing, sometimes sobbing, and sometimes a faint voice answering a question from the tutor.

I think she may have been Mrs. Gladys Yang, the British-born wife of a Chinese national, who was working in Peking as a literary translator, and was arrested some time about September, 1968.

Although each prisoner was given exercises alone, I began to build up a dossier on some of the others in the "Remolding Prison".

My clues as to their identities were some old envelopes which I found in the box-room when emptying rubbish. They bore American stamps. Two of the names were Anglo-Saxon—Major Philip Smith and John Downey, and one was French—Richard Fecteau.

Major Smith was a U.S. Air Force pilot who had been shot down over Chinese territory when his aircraft strayed out of Vietnamese air space in 1951.

Downey and Fecteau, civilians with the U.S. Army during the Korean War, had been captured 18 years before when the aircraft in which they were hitching a lift was shot down. Another American, Hugh Redmond, was also on board. Downey and Redmond were sentenced to life imprisonment, and Fecteau to 20 years—all on charges of spying.

I think I saw both Downey and Fecteau. When cleaning the corridor I used to get an occasional glimpse into the cells by lingering at cell doors waiting for the breeze—it was a very draughty prison—to lift the little curtain which hung over the observation peep-holes. I was really shocked by the sight of the two men I took to be Downey and Fecteau. They sat in their cells gazing into space like listless old beggars; the effects of years of brainwashing and unknown tortures were only too plain.

Yet little things showed that those men still had some spirit left. One days the guards, in letting me go to the the lavatory at the end of the corridor, made a mistake in their timing. On my way back I saw one of the men mopping away at the stone floor of the corridor. He was moving slowly, and with obvious difficulty; but as I passed he lifted his head just enough to look me in the eye. And he winked.

The cells were fitted with loudspeakers which would occasionally be tuned to Radio Peking for an hour-long

English language programme of propaganda. One morning the man at the controls accidentally tuned in to the Voice of America. He kept on that station long enough for us to hear a few sentences. Cheers came from the cells.

Each of us had to take turns mopping out the corridor. One day I heard someone at work near my cell door. He slowed down when right outside and I heard an American voice say, *"Hi, George Watt?"* I suppose my name was known because a report of my trial had been carried in the English language *Peking Review* which we were sometimes permitted to read.

"Yes," I replied. . . . "I'm British."

He started to whistle *From the Halls of Montezuma* and I replied with *Land of Hope and Glory*. From then on, we built up a "song link" between us. Sometimes I whistled or sang *Rule Britannia* or the National Anthem, and the Americans would reply with *The Stars and Stripes or Wings Over the Ocean*. But we seldom managed to get through more than a few bars before guards were bellowing for silence, and hammering at the cell doors.

One day I heard a rather hard, rasping American voice shouting: "You goddam little bastards don't scare me. . . ." Then the guards began yelling, and there was thumping on a door.

I recognized the voice as that of the man I had identified as the pilot, Major Smith. He was a defiant man—defiant to the point of recklessness. One afternoon, on my way to a brainwashing session, I heard the voice again. He called: "George, don't take any crap off them."

During all my time in the Remolding Center, I must report that I was never beaten up. But Major Smith was; his outright defiance was clearly too much for the Chinese.

One crisp spring morning he called out: "Hell I want to go for a walk. Do you hear that? A walk. I want a walk."

I shouted back to him: "Do you want to borrow my file?" And his answering laughter bellowed down the corridor.

That morning we were due to receive our monthly soap supply, but it hadn't arrived.

131

Major Smith's voice shattered the calm: "Why is there no goddam soap? Do you hear me, you buzzards? I want soap . . . soap . . . I want some goddam SOAP."

Astonishingly, this produced results. The soap arrived later that day, and I heard the bars being piled up on the corridor tables from which, one by one, we would be allowed out to collect it.

While I waited my turn, commotion broke out. From the corridor I could hear running feet, Major Smith swearing at the top of his lungs, and the guards chattering and barking orders.

I dragged my chair up to the cell door and stood on it to peer through the tiny glass fanlight above. There was the major, three quarters of the way down the corridor, standing at a table piled high with soap. He was throwing the bars with all his might at the guards and yelling: "You know what you can do with your goddam soap."

At first the guards—there were three of them—huddled down at the far end, apparently thrown off balance, as most Chinese Communists seem to be when the unexpected happens. And still the soap bars kept hurtling down.

Then the guards, joined by reinforcements, advanced slowly. The major was undismayed. He counted them as they stalked him . . . "One . . . two . . . three . . . four. . . ."

Up to 15. Then he roared: "Fifteen of you, eh? Fifteen. . . ? It'll take another fifteen of you to ge me back in my cell."

They jumped on him, and the major disappeared beneath, punching, kicking, clawing guards. But he was still fighting mad and they had quite a job to pitch him back into his cell.

The corridor was like a skating rink with all that litter of soap chips, and I was detailed to clear up the mess. As I mopped away I was thinking, "Poor old Smithy, he must have gone off his rocker."

Edging near his cell, I heard him coughing and gasping as he recovered from the beating. He must have heard me moving for suddenly I heard his voice: "Whatever you do, you mustn't let them get you down."

That made me change my mind about the major, Smithy had not gone mad—he was just fighting his own battle in his own way.

*   *   *

The summer of 1968 was hot and sticky, and I was badly bitten by mosquitoes. But when the tutor saw me scratching he was moved to a most unexpected act of kindness—he gave me a fly-swatter.

I had decided by this time that my only chance of getting out of the Remolding Center was to appear to fall in with the wishes of the Chinese, so I pretended to be a model pupil of Communism. I studied every book they gave me as if my life depended on it . . . as indeed it may well have done.

It was in November 1968 that I was allowed to write the first letter to my wife since being detained in August 1967, but what a trouble I had getting that letter away. The letter was brought back every one or two weeks and I was told to "change that line", or asked, "What does that mean?" After I had explained I would inevitably be told to change it.

Just to give an example, I had originally written: "I'm having a nice time and the food is good—tell it to the Marines." That resulted in a two-hour grilling on exactly what it was I wanted to tell the Marines, and I was eventually told that it was not necessary to tell the Marines about the prison food.

I was January 1969 before the letter was finally passed as suitable for posting.

On another occasion there was trouble following the arrival of a letter from my wife. It was soon after the introduction of the new postal codes and inside my letter I found a slip of paper with the words "Post Code—GL 51 5JQ". The letter was brought in to me by my tutor, accompanied by two or three political commissars, who wanted to know what the letters and numbers on the slip of paper meant.

133

I explained that this was the postal code, and that the idea was that letters should be delivered more quickly.

His eyes gleamed with triumph.

"You will not affix those code letters to your next communication home. Your wife has slipped up this time, hasn't she?"

Although I knew this could be serious for me, I was having difficulty in stifling laughter.

"You admit," he said, sternly now, "that those are code letters?"

Meekly I replied, "Yes, I suppose so."

Now he snarled. "Good, good. You are cornered—at last. Make your confessions now. Admit your crimes. Tell us where your letters *really* go. Explain what this code means."

The more I tried to explain how innocuous a postal code was, the more he insisted that I was lying.

Then, incredibly, he thundered that unless I made a full confession immediately, my sentence would be increased.

But I persisted in declaring my innocence and eventually they left, though not without adding that the matter would be investigated at high level.

Two weeks later, the political commissars returned—smiling. They said that they had been in touch with London, and the postal code was indeed genuine. They pointed out, almost apologetically, that they couldn't be too careful—they must always guard themselves against the schemings of British Imperialists and their agents.

The Chinese had refused to supply me with any clothing, and it was not long before the seat of my trousers wore away completely. It was dead of winter and I was freezing; my backside seemed to be under a permanent anaesthetic.

I had sent off to the Red Cross to beg for a pair of trousers but winter 1968 had turned into summer 1969—into blazing heat—before the parcel arrived. It contained a pair of heavy, thick workman's trousers.

I received my first Red Cross parcel towards the end of 1968; there was tinned meat, sweets, chocolate, biscuits, cheese, tinned fruit, and American cigarettes in tins.

The Red Cross parcels normally contained tins of food, but the big problem was to get at the contents, for while some of the tins had lids that could easily be pried open, others—containing soup or beans—needed a can opener. If I gave them to the guard to open I could be pretty certain that was the last I'd see of them. Though there were some honest guards who operated on the Communist principle that one person ought not receive more than another. It was either that or they were reluctant to pilfer the contents of a can in case they were caught—with dire consequences.

I can recall sitting in my cell in winter, shivering in my threadbare clothes, with snow and sleet swirling in through the broken window, and reading on the label of a can of soup, "Directions for serving. To retain the full flavor, empty the contents into a saucepan, and see that it reaches boiling point. Then simmer gently for a few minutes."

The instructions sometimes insisted on my having a greased casserole dish to put in an oven at Mark 7. So it was rather unfortunate that my entire culinary equipment consisted of a chipped mug, with a tiny hole in the bottom—which meant that when drinking water I had to keep a finger firmly over the hole.

I did ask Jo, in my letter home, to tell the Red Cross that I had no cooking facilities, but the Chinese insisted on that information being deleted.

The parcels had to be opened in front of the tutor and two guards and I then had to make a list of the contents, and sign a receipt saying that they had arrived intact. After that the Chinese would help themselves to anything they fancied, and tell me: "We will take this away for testing."

Once I asked: "Why not select the items for testing first and I'll make out a receipt for what remains?"

But the tutor said: "No. Receipt first, then the testing." I knew, of course, that they were eating the stuff themselves. One day a bar of chocolate designed for "testing" was unwrapped, broken into squares, and offered to me.

Cigarettes caused problems because they were marked *For use of AMERICAN FORCES only*.

I was interrogated for days about those cigarettes.

"This", I was told, "proves your true connections and identity with American Intelligence. Those cigarettes are not for ordinary people. They cannot be bought in shops."

Then I was ordered: "Come—make your confession."

* * *

Shortly after the American cigarette episode, I experienced a strange act of kindness. At night only one guard was on duty, and there was one particular one who, until the Soviet quit China, had been a Russian interpreter.

When on duty he would sometimes slip into my cell and, with a few words of Russian and Chinese, we would manage a slight chat.

I showed him photographs of my family and he would say: "Nice children."

One night, he pointed to the photographs, then to me, and said: *"You go two years."*

I had no way of knowing whether this would prove to be true. I did know that I was not being comforted or mollycoddled. I was never given a blanket and in winter I froze. My underclothes, which I washed every week, were nothing more than a few holes held together by threads of cotton.

But towards the middle of 1969 I detected signs that made me think I might be gaining headway. The food became slightly better and the lectures in the tutor's office became more positive. They obviously thought I was becoming good revolutionary material.

They showed me films of how to make petrol bombs, stone bombs, and nail bombs. How was I to guess then that nail bombs would be used in my native Ulster against British troops in November, 1970?

There were films, demonstrating how a Communist agent should infiltrate poor areas and trade unions to stir up trouble.

"A clever agitator," said the tutor, "can do more damage to a factory than an aircraft dropping a bomb on the roof."

* * *

Early in 1970 the tutor was quite excited when he came to my cell. He held up a newspaper . . . "I have heard some wonderful news about your native Ulster," he said. "Bernadette Devlin was presented with the key of New York by the mayor, and this was in turn presented to the Black Panthers. That is a great gesture of defiance at the American lackeys.

"Northern Ireland can be compared to the mountain range where Mao Tse-tung set out on his long march to take over China.

"In Ulster, the revolution to take over Britain has started. People such as Bernadette Devlin are lighting the prairie fires which will spread to Liverpool and Glasgow, where the large Irish population will join the underprivileged immigrants. . . . It will be the start of THE LIBERATION OF BRITAIN."

To the Chinese, Bernadette Devlin was quite a heroine. So was Reg Birch, the chairman of a Maoist group of British Communists.

He was mentioned in glowing terms several times, and it was obvious that the Chinese looked on him as the future leader of Britain . . . and not in the too distant future.

Things soon began speeding up. I was taken to the tutor's room every day and told that, as I appeared to be sincerely atoning for my crimes, I was being regarded as "good revolutionary material". But I was warned that I must be prepared "to fight for the revolution".

On 25 March, 1970, I saw a doctor for the first time. It was for a blood test. Three days later, I was X-rayed, and on 31 March I was given an anti-flu injection, and told that I would be allowed an hour's exercise in the yard every day.

A two-line entry in my diary for 14 April reads: "My little son's first day at school—Out soon?"

* * *

One day, around that time, I was given a fried egg for lunch. It was a trifle burned, but it tasted delicious.

Then small chunks of roast pork began to be served with

137

my rice. Once I was given about a dozen chips. Then little treats began to crop up . . . a piece of fried fish, small slices of ham. I was being fattened up for freedom.

On the morning of 30 July, 1970, I stared in amazement at my breakfast. They had given me four boiled eggs and some grey bread. It couldn't be a mistake . . . they don't make that kind of mistake. And the guards were smiling . . . yes, actually smiling.

Lunch was two half-inch thick steaks, measuring about three by four inches each, with cabbage and rice. But still the Chinese said nothing.

I opened up the end of a toothpaste tube, squeezed it dry, and slipped in my fourpenny stamp with the Queen's head on it. I would not leave that.

Then it occurred to me that I had been too optimistic. But no; soon after lunch the tutor said: "We are going to have a little ceremony. Bring your Red Book, and follow me."

I was taken to a large hall which I hadn't seen before. Assembled there were the Prison Director of Discipline, political commissars, members of the Public Security Bureau, and some Red Guards.

The director stood up, looked at me, and said: "We are to announce an act of clemency on your behalf." He then read out a detailed history of my case. It lasted for half an hour.

Finally came what I had been waiting and hoping for . . . "George Watt, British Imperialist spy, you are to be immediately released because you have accepted our remolding."

I did not dare move, or even change the expression on my face. But they gathered round me, clapping and smiling. They appeared to be very proud of me.

"You have done very well," they said. "When you return to Britain you must always remember the great leniency we have shown you. We should have executed you but you are now free.

"In Britain, it is likely that some friends of China will contact you. When this happens, you must do whatever you can to aid the Revolution.

138

"Always remember that you owe us your life. You are in our debt."

I inclined my head, and let them assume that this indicated agreement.

That night, escorted by two guards, I caught the train for Canton. It took two days and nights, stopping at almost every station on the way. I learned on that journey why, before leaving jail, they had given me a dinner of two steaks, three fried eggs, chips, fried tomatoes, and lettuce. Throughout the entire journey we had nothing to eat but dry grey bread.

After an overnight stay at Canton Government rest house, we caught another train which took us to the Hong Kong border. It was 2 August, 1970.

I stepped into the Chinese Customs shed and found that they had one more dig to take at me. The Customs officer found a fully used cheque book of stubs in my case.

I was told that as I had not declared this when entering China, I would have to wait while it was checked. I waited for two hours, during which there were the usual hints that I might have to return to Peking . . . that I had committed other serious crimes . . . and would have to be held for further investigation.

I didn't trust myself to open my mouth. I just sat there and prayed. Finally, I was told that everything had been cleared up, and I could go.

They pointed to the border. Over the bridge I could see the Union Jack. I wanted to run like mad towards it.

It was not until I heard a British police officer say: "Good afternoon, Mr. Watt. . . . Welcome back . . ." that I knew I was safe, at last.

But it didn't really feel like home until I was asked if there was anything I wanted—was I hungry or thirsty?

Yes, indeed.

"Give me a Guinness!" I said joyfully.

Once the excitement had died down a bit I remember glancing down at the jade ring on my finger—the souvenir of my stay in China, which I wear to this day. I had bought the ring with the money I had saved during my stay in the Ideological Remolding Center, for although I

139

had had to pay my air-fare from Peking to Lanchow for my trial, the "remolding" had been provided at the expense of the People's Republic of China.

At that point I couldn't stop my thoughts wandering back to the friends I had left behind, those who were still in prison in China.

All I had been able to do before leaving was to whisper through the observation window of Major Smith's cell door:

"Keep your chin up, Smithy!"

THE END

Author welcomes correspondence.
Inquiries and gifts for the underground church
may be sent to:
Jesus to the Communist World
P. O. Box 11
Glendale, CA 91209

APPENDIX I

Brainwashing

In the previous chapter I described my life in the Ideological Remolding Center, but said little about Chinese attempts to brainwash me; it is this aspect of my imprisonment with which I shall here be concerned.

From the time I first heard that the Chinese had sentenced me to three years' imprisonment I realized only too well that I should have to fight a desperate battle of wits with them. If at the end of three years I hadn't convinced them that I was at least sympathetic towards Chinese Communism, they were sure to discover some further trumped-up charges to keep me in prison, perhaps for the rest of my life.

I realized that the battle of wits I'd fought with them during my six months' interrogation would be child's play compared with the mighty, concentrated battle about to be staged.

I took stock of myself. I had a working, lower-middle-class background, and had started my career as an apprentice—a manual worker. The Chinese are very class conscious, I thought, so I ought to be able to capitalize on this.

I couldn't help think, though, not unkindly, that von Xylander, the German who was being interrogated in Lanchow, was at a decided disadvantage with his title and aristocratic background. At least I hadn't that burden to bear.

I also had another advantage in that I was convinced—absolutely and immovably—that they would never succeed in brainwashing me.

I must, in all fairness, mention that both in the Soviet Union and in China I had read much of the Communist theory which they love to stuff down the throats of visiting foreigners. And the theory is not unreasonable. Indeed, people who haven't travelled might well be impressed by it.

I decided, therefore, no matter how much Communist

141

theory you give me to study, at least there is something I will know—and that is that I must be honest with myself. I mustn't be deceived into believing what *should* happen, but must keep in the forefront of my mind what in fact *does* happen.

I must remember that I am not, fundamentally, concerned with theory, but with stark reality. One doesn't need to be a political genius to realize that Communism doesn't do much good for the ordinary man in a Communist country.

My natural attitude of mind, the need to face facts and to be honest with myself, was, I felt, a strong weapon with which to combat their insidious poison. Then, too, I am an Ulster Unionist and my pride in Northern Ireland's connection with Great Britain—call it British brainwashing, if you like—has made me completely impervious to any assault by Communist ideology.

To prepare for my battle of wits against the Chinese, I reviewed the two opposing forces. I thought about their disadvantages, and I thought about all my advantages. I looked upon this as the greatest challenge I had faced. I decided to let them think that they were obtaining mastery over my mind. What I had to do was to develop a two-channel line of thinking. I had to absorb their political theory—even become an expert at it—then switch it off and on at appropriate times.

In other words, go with the political commissar and discuss Communism in all apparent seriousness; even discuss it with more ability and confidence than he. Then, back in my cell, have a quiet chuckle, turn it off, like a transistor radio, and say "It's all a load of damned nonsense. It doesn't happen in practice!"

The political commissar I was dealing with spoke very good English. I don't know if this was part of his job, but he was always most pleasant to me. He did not ill-treat me, and obviously set out to win my confidence. In all fairness, I must put on record that he was one of the few Communists I could really tolerate. He behaved at all times in a gentlemanly fashion and I can only speak highly about his behavior. It may all have been part of an elaborate front to win my confidence, but I rather think not.

When he brought me my first book, he said, "I'd like you to study this, and give me your truthful opinion of what you think about it."

I read the book, although I found concentration most difficult with the prisoners above me making such a noise. They were chained night and day, and when they dragged themselves over the floor to the lavatory bucket, the scraping was horrifying. Then came the sound of urine splashing into the bucket. The whole thing became unnerving.

Eventually, the interpreter returned to ask me what I thought of the book.

Calmly and deliberately I said, "I think it is a superb book to read and study. I have learned a great deal from it."

He nodded approval, and went out smiling, obviously satisfied.

I was, in the circumstances, speaking the truth. It was indeed a most appropriate book for me to study in that particular situation. As I've said, my reading was continually being disturbed by the people above, and across the flyleaf of the book was written:

> *Throw off your chains,*
> *You have nothing to lose but your chains.*

What more suitable book could one read in a Communist prison?

I think that most Irishmen have a built-in sense of humor. Perhaps it can sometimes be described as peculiar, but it certainly helped me to withstand the Communist drear. I am sure that this sense of humor kept me from being downcast.

During my early days in the political prison I continued to plan my campaign of resistance. My thoughts kept drifting back to the Africa which I love, as they still so often do. I remembered, years before, speaking to a Christian missionary, who told me that the majority of his congregation dabbled in the native cult of ju-ju. I was horrified to

143

hear this, and asked him why he didn't try to put a stop to it. The missionary replied that it was a useful way of conveying the Christian message to the Africans. He was prepared to turn a blind eye because the natives felt that being members of the Church and having a stake in ju-ju on the side, they had a two-way chance, a foot in both camps.

I saw a lesson for myself in this—I resolved to continue to say my nightly prayers, and at the same time to make a determined effort to study the Chinese Communist ideology. But as I have already pointed out, I had no intention whatsoever of being "remolded" in the sense that my captors meant; my efforts in this direction served only one end—to enable me to persuade the Chinese that they had succeeded in brainwashing me, so that I should regain my freedom.

I was called to the tutor's office for a lecture on Mao's brand of Marxism-Leninism once a week. He always asked me questions and gave me "homework" to do in my cell, which meant that I had to write reports on the lectures and on what I had learned from my reading of *The Selected Works of Mao Tse-tung* and *Quotations from Chairman Mao*.

The cells in the prison were fitted with loudspeakers, which were sometimes turned to Radio Peking for an hour-long programme of propaganda in English. The one which most fascinated me was entitled *Victory in Vietnam*, broadcast every Saturday morning. It always contained exaggerated reports of serious American losses; American troops were always falling back. Indeed if the total losses inflicted on Americans were to be believed, the United States would have been completely depopulated.

It is, of course, common for commanders to exaggerate their victories and minimize their losses. I remember listening to "Lord Haw Haw"—William Joyce—broadcasting from Germany during the Second World War. If he reported that the British had lost twelve aircraft, and the Nazis only three, one could conclude that the score was even.

The Chinese Communists went one better than the

Nazis. They weren't content with exaggerating American losses, and minimizing their own; they just didn't admit any losses. It was all victory after victory; defeat didn't enter into the picture.

The Chinese Communists certainly do not hold American soldiers in high esteem, though I must say here that from my own experience, these are opinions which I cannot share.

The Chinese despise the Americans first and foremost because "you cannot give an American boy a rifle and a bag of rice and send him out into the jungle with the order —Go get yourself an enemy. He would end up getting lost, or bitten by a snake."

The affluent society, they feel, is not the right training ground to produce tough, disciplined fighting men. They contend that the average American soldier is useless on his feet; he has to be transported to and from the scene of combat. Since he is so much cosseted, he lacks stamina and the determination to kill.

Another weakness of Americans, say the Chinese, is that they don't like the close hand-to-hand fighting. But the Chinese, they argue, could never be completely conquered. They appreciate that Chinese cities could be destroyed by nuclear weapons, but at the end of the day the country would have to be occupied by weapon-carrying troops— who would be at the mercy of the Chinese populace.

Although they are certain they will not be at war with the United States, the Chinese are not resigned to imagining that they will live in peace indefinitely. Indeed, they feel that they must fight another war; Chairman Mao has concentrated on training their minds to this end.

In discussions with Chinese guards and commissars, I learned that their minds are conditioned to the inevitable —a war with their arch-enemies, the Japanese.

An important point here is that the Chinese Communists have tremendous admiration for Japanese soldiers. I formed the impression that the Chinese expect to be in full conflict with Japan in the 1980's. They are resigned to losing their cities, but they will continue to follow their old pattern of controlling the countryside and the lines of communication. An invading army would be hemmed in to numerous city enclaves. They would then be prepared to play a waiting game, and sit the enemy out.

The Western reader will probably find this difficult to believe. But we are here dealing with the Oriental mind. They decided to build the Great Wall: it took them two centuries, but to them, decades pass like the twinkling of an eye.

My tutor asked me one day: "Suppose your country was being invaded, and you had a mine along a road, which you could detonate. Approaching, you could see a massive enemy tank, and behind, a truckload of infantry carrying only small arms. What would you go for?"

I said that, obviously, I'd go for the tank, because that had the greater potential for causing damage.

He said, "Yes, that is how Western military commanders think. But a Chinese would let the tank through, and destroy the truck . . . because this is in accordance with Chairman Mao's thought that people are more important than things. The tank could be replaced, but it is not so easy to replace the enemy's trained soldiers. And to destroy the tank has no effect back behind the lines in the enemy's home country; destroy the soldiers, and you send back an anti-war message into many homes. This takes psychological warfare deep into enemy country; an aspect that Western military men do not seem to consider."

* * *

And so the weeks passed; my political instructor continued to call at my cell, or summon me to a special room at the south end of the corridor for our "discussions". Many clear-cut patterns began to emerge and I started to recognize these as Chinese Communist hard-core policy. Tremendous importance was attached to "propaganda", or, as Mao would say, "doing work in the ideological sphere". Not only propaganda for Chinese Communists, but propaganda to be carried out on an international scale.

I think it is worth stressing here the difference, as I see it between Soviet and Chinese ideology.

The Soviet Communists believe that the two opposing political systems can exist peaceably side by side. The Chinese do not believe that this can be so; eventually one must conquer the other. Mao himself in his own "Thoughts" states that either the East Wind prevails over the West, or the West Wind over the East.

The Russian Communists believe that if Communists form the majority of the electorate in Western democracies, they can come to power via the ballot box.

On the other hand, Chinese Communists believe that this can never take place; they can come to power only by violent revolution—Mao's own words are, "Political power grows out of the barrel of a gun". The Chinese are determined that their special brand of Maoism will conquer the entire world; their sights are set on global domination. To achieve this end, they employ Mao's tactics of using the countryside to surround the cities on an international scale. The cities of the world are the highly industrialized nations; the countrysides of the world are the underdeveloped nations.

The idea of the Chinese Communists is to cause agitation and internal strife in underdeveloped countries as an indirect way of bringing pressure to bear on the developed countries. In this they concentrate on certain key areas. To take one example, in Africa the European settlers have by sheer hard work developed South Africa and adjoining regions, whereas in Tanzania and Zambia, the natives have not yet demonstrated their ability to follow suit. The Chinese will use these regions to foment unrest, and use racism as a cover for their real purpose—their Communist activities.

My instructor used to say, "A clever agitator can do more damage in a factory than a bomb through the roof."

An agitator does not have to be a strike leader—indeed, he may be wiser not to be the leader. There is usually a loud-mouthed malcontent in every workshop, often living beyond his means and thus an easy victim to be manipulated by a cunning agitator.

The attitude of the agitator is, "You tell the boss where he gets off. Go on, don't be afraid . . . I'll back you up."

147

So, when strikes do occur, the leaders are not usually members of the Communist Party. This is well known; but what is not so well known is that they are puppets—often without their own knowledge. They are not even aware how deftly the strings are being pulled by Communists.

I well remember being told at one particular lecture that students were encouraged to act as "outside agitators", under the slogan of "Students and workers unite". This is not usually very effective, since the students do not themselves have to earn their keep, haven't the responsibility of bringing up a family and don't pay Income Tax. So when they go along to a strike and try to incite, the workers don't as a rule, fall for these tactics.

My tutor was almost invariably pleasant to me, and nearly always showed a smiling face. It was obvious, however, that this outwardly cordial manner was designed only to help him put over his political message. The Chinese attempt to brainwash me was not a pleasant experience, but it taught me quite a lot. By listening closely to the lectures and reading the so-called "independent literature", I became acutely aware of the terrible dangers with which we in the Western world are faced. We don't realize how the long fingers of subversion stretch into every walk of life, and manipulate the disgruntled, the immature, and the social misfits.

APPENDIX II

Businessmen in China

During late July, 1968, when I was settling into prison life, my interpreter came in with the weekly copy of *Peking Review*, an English language propaganda sheet.

It was always full of letters of praise, from England, Canada, Germany, but never from a full address which could be pinpointed. In other words, it appeared that the people who were so proudly praising China didn't want their true name and address to be disclosed.

I was deeply suspicious of the whole set-up so I kept back copies and, during the long hours in my cell, I studied the letters carefully. There was a distinct similarity in the style of writing; a letter from Italy would be virtually the same one that had been published months before, allegedly coming from Denmark. It was not long before I was firmly convinced that those letters, or most of them, originated in Peking.

On this particular day in July, the interpreter was jubilant. He pointed to the *Peking Review* in triumph . . . the Great Chinese People, guided by Mao's Thoughts, and exercising high vigilance, had punished my Imperialist weapon-manufacturing masters.

I looked at him, wondering to myself, "What the devil is he raving about now?"

He told me that the Chinese had dealt "a heavy blow" against Vickers.

They had been found guilty of fraud against the Chinese people, and the Vickers-Zimmer personnel still in China were to be kicked out of the country, and the company had been instructed to pay an indemnity of £650,000 (sterling).

He went on to read out a long list of "crimes" committed by Vickers against the Chinese.

Looking straight at me, he announced that Vickers had sent many spies into China—"and you, George Watt, stole a large quantity of important Intelligence, concerning China's military, political and economic affairs".

I was familiar with this style. It would never be merely "Intelligence", but "a *large* quantity of *important* Intelligence".

Then he added something that nearly sent me into hysterics. Solemnly, he informed me that the Vickers directors had been invited to leave London and travel to Peking—to be placed on trial and to answer for their crimes. They had refused to attend for trial. Thus proving, he assured me, that they were, beyond all doubt, guilty. If they had been confident of their innocence, he intoned, they would, of course, have been eager to come out to Peking.

With an air of triumph, he threw down the *Peking Review*, and marched out of the cell, banging the door behind him.

I was stunned, but it turned out that the report in the newspaper was not this time merely Communist propaganda and distortion of events. The company I had been working for, first in the Soviet Union, and then in Red China, Vickers-Zimmer Ltd., really had been found guilty of fraud by a court in Peking, and sentence had subsequently been pronounced, though in the absence of the directors of the company who, not surprisingly, had declined the invitation to attend the trial.

The best way of giving a clear picture of how the Chinese dealt with the case is to reproduce below part of the official verdict, which was read out at the time by a representative of the Peking Municipal Intermediate People's Court:

"On 3 July, 1968, the Peking Municipal Intermediate People's Court held a mass meeting at which the great red banner of Mao Tse-tung's thought was held high, and the verdict in the fraud case of the British Vickers-Zimmer Ltd., was announced. The verdict was read out in the absence of the defendant, Vickers-Zimmer Ltd., which dared not appear at the meeting.

"To safeguard the security and socialist construction of our country and the fruits of victory of the great proletarian cultural revolution, the Peking Municipal Intermediate People's Court decreed:

"The contract concerning a plant, signed on 25 November, 1964, between the defendant Vickers-Zimmer Ltd., and the China National Technical Import Corporation is to be annulled immediately as of the date of the present judgment; personnel of the Vickers-Zimmer Ltd. still in China must leave the country within ten days of the date of the present judgment; and the Vickers-Zimmer Ltd. shall pay an indemnity of 650,000 British pounds to the China National Technical Import Corporation for economic losses suffered by the latter.

150

"This just verdict fully demonstrated the great might of the dictatorship of the proletariat of our country.

"When the meeting opened, the revolutionary masses present read in unison the great leader Chairman Mao's teaching:

"The imperialists and domestic reactionaries will certainly not take their defeat lying down, and they will struggle to the last ditch. After there is peace and order throughout the country, they will still engage in sabotage and create disturbances in various ways and will try every day and every minute to stage a come-back. This is inevitable and beyond all doubt, and under no circumstances must we relax our vigilance."

The Chinese seized this opportunity to mention the matter of my own case and trial, and tried to make it appear as if Vickers-Zimmer had used the construction of the plant merely as a cover for espionage activities:

"In the course of more than three years, while the contract was under execution, abundant facts showed that the defendant had no intention of fulfilling the contract, and had been deliberately perpetuating a fraud. Among the so-called technical personnel it had sent to China, some are incompetent, while others were spies disguised as technical personnel.

"Before the spy George Watt came to China, he had been assigned the task of collecting intelligence by P. F. W. Jay, a responsible member of the defendant company.

"During his stay in China, George Watt stole a large quantity of important intelligence about China's military, political, and economic affairs, and the great proletarian cultural revolution, thus rendering active serve to the British imperialist policy of aggression and opposing the People's Republic of China.

"The above offender had already been sentenced by the intermediate people's court of Lanchow in Kansu Province.

"Another so-called engineer, Peter Deckart, who also

carried out espionage activities in China, had been expelled from the country by our public security authorities."

As if that were not enough, the verdict went on to point out that we—the engineers who had been sent out to China—were pretty useless at the actual job of construction:

"It was stipulated in the contract that the defendant Vickers-Zimmer Ltd. undertook to supply the China National Technical Import Corporation with the most up-to-date design and techniques, the best equipment and materials, and ensure the realization of the guaranteed values as stated in the contract.

"But facts have proved that the defendant had not grasped the main techniques concerning the contracted plant, and had repeatedly resorted to chicanery.

"In addition, with regard to delivery of technical documents, the supply of equipment and materials, and arrangements for trainees and other matters, the defendant had always defrauded by resorting to such tricks as procrastination, shirking responsibility, and flat denials."

In conclusion it was declared that:

"The criminal activities of the defendant Vickers-Zimmer Ltd. were deliberate political and economic sabotage and fraud, under the camouflage of trade, against the People's Republic of China, in an attempt to endanger China's security and undermine its socialist construction."

At this juncture all those present at the meeting enthusiastically applauded in support of the solemn judgment of the Peking Municipal Intermediate People's Court. The revolutionary masses pointed out:

"China is a great socialist country exercising the dictatorship of the proletariat. The Chinese people wish to have friendly co-operation with the people of all coun-

152

tries in the world and develop international trade on the basis of equality and mutual benefit, but they will never allow any enemy to take advantage of this to sabotage and make trouble in China."

Then the revolutionary masses started shouting:

"Down with U.S. imperialism! Down with British imperialism! Long live the dictatorship of the proletariat! Long live all-round victory in the great proletarian cultural revolution" and "Long live the great leader Chairman Mao! A long, long life to him!"

At the end of the meeting, everyone sang *Sailing the Seas Depends on the Helmsman.*

*　　*　　*

It is certainly not my intention here to pass judgment on political decisions, but in the light of recent events— President Nixon's visit to Peking, the promise of better relations with Red China, and the optimistic hopes which have been raised with regard to the future, I should like to point out that there is a lesson to be learned from my own experiences with the Chinese people.

I have related the tale of the difficulties I faced whilst working in China, and my imprisonment on trumped-up charges of spying; I have shown that the Communist Chinese are prepared to stoop to anything that serves their ends, as the Vickers-Zimmer case demonstrates.

The directors of the company would clearly have been made to travel to Peking to answer the charges of fraud, and I feel sure that the Chinese were convinced all along that they would not appear to defend themselves. The whole affair was craftily thought out so that the Chinese had a first-class excuse for confiscating the synthetic fibres plant as a "fine" against the directors of Vickers-Zimmer —once the plant had been almost completed and they had all the information necessary to put it into commission.

The lesson to be learned, then, is that it is impossible to

carry out trade with Red China on a normal basis; if business is to be done, those concerned should insist on cash paid on the nail—if not in advance. It seems to me, though, that there is no one hundred per cent foolproof way of doing business with them.

Even the Vickers-Zimmer case was not an isolated incident, for similar charges of "fraud" and "cheating" were brought against both a German and a French firm, and their plants were likewise confiscated. During my own stay in China I saw numerous factories which had been left unfinished by the Russians when they withdrew their China aid programme in about 1960—after they found that it was impossible to deal with the Chinese on any reasonable basis.

Incidentally, the Chinese had made no effort whatsoever to complete the buildings after they had been abandoned; when I saw them there were trees growing out of the windows and through the roof. This in itself, this lax attitude to work, is indicative of the topsy-turvy world of Chinese Communism.

It brings to mind the times whilst I was working on the site at Lanchow, when I would look out of my office window to find that the Chinese workers had disappeared without a word. They would suddenly decide to hold a meeting, at which one or other of them would read out of *The Thoughts of Mao*.

To come back to the question of trade with China, the reader may say to himself, this is not something that concerns me greatly. But that is not quite accurate, since when things go wrong, as they did in the case of Vickers-Zimmer, it is ultimately the British tax-payer who foots the bill. The plant constructed in Lanchow was worth about three million pounds, and the firm would probably have been reimbursed for the major portion of its losses under the Export Credits Guarantee scheme. Since the revenue for this must come from the pocket of the tax-payer it is not surprising if, when the full realization of his involvement dawns on him, he is prompted to question the wisdom of seeking to do trade with Communist countries such as Red China.

APPENDIX III

CHINA
(DETAINED BRITISH SUBJECTS)

Motion made, and Question proposed, That this House
do now adjourn.—[*Mr. McBride.*]

9.55 p.m.

Mr. Stanley R. McMaster (Belfast, East): Mr. Speaker,
I thank you for this opportunity of raising the case of
George Watt and others and of drawing the attention of
the House to the plight of this gentleman and at least 12
other British citizens and some of their families who have
been detained by the Chinese. Mr. Watt is an engineer who
was employed by Vickers-Zimmer, a British company
which has been engaged since 1966 in the erection of a
polypropylene plant in Lanchow in China. The plant was
commissioned by Techimport, a Chinese trading organiza-
tion. Mr. Watt, a Belfast man, was employed by the company as an engineer and along with one or two other
engineers was at the site in Lanchow supervising the construction of this plant.

His wife joined him in China in July last year and they
spent two months together there. She left in September and
shortly after leaving Peking she was searched on her way
through Shanghai and some family photographs were taken
from her luggage. She was fully searched, she told me.
The photographs were ordinary family ones, all of which
had been taken in China in the presence of the Chinese
interpreter who accompanied them, and none of which
were in any way of a nature that might have infringed
security or military secrecy.

However, following the searching of Mrs. Watt, Mr.
Watt was placed under house arrest in his hotel in Peking.
Later, I believe, he was taken back to the hotel in Lan-

chow where he had stayed when he was working with Vickers-Zimmer and kept under arrest in his room in that hotel. I am told by members of the company that none of his colleagues or friends in the company were permitted to see him or speak to him. The only communication they received was when he sent bills for his food to the company asking that they should be paid by the company and when he asked that his effects should be sent back to Britain. Except for those notes, no other communication was received and none of his friends in Lanchow working for Vickers-Zimmer or other British companies there were allowed to see or to talk to him, nor was he able to write to his wife or family in this country.

The British Mission in Peking, which was informed of the situation, made attempts to get in touch with him but it also was unsuccessful. The Chinese authorities did not allow any access to Mr. Watt between the middle of September, when he was placed under arrest, and March this year when the world was informed by the New China News Agency that he had been charged and tried for espionage, convicted and sentenced to three years imprisonment. No other information about the trial was given to the British Mission in spite of the representations it made to the Chinese. No British consular official was able to attend the trial. No note of the evidence against Mr. Watt was forwarded to the British Mission in Peking. Neither Mr. Watt's friends in the company nor the British Foreign Office know anything about the proceedings at the trial. All that we know—

It being Ten o'clock, the Motion for the Adjournment of the House lapsed, without Question put.

Motion made, and Question proposed, That this House do now adjourn.—[*Mr. McBride.*]

10.0 p.m.

Mr. McMaster: All that we know is that there were two releases from the New China News Agency, one on 12th March of this year which reported Mr. Watt's address and the later one which reported his trial. This is all the information which anyone has had about Mr. Watt since September last. Since his trial and his reported conviction by the New China News Agency, no diplomatic access has been granted to him. So far as we know, no letters from his wife have reached him. His wife tells me that she has written to him but that the letters have been returned through the firm. None has been received by Mr. Watt. No letters from Mr. Watt have reached his wife or his family. They are in complete ignorance as to his state

EXTRACT FROM HANSARD
PARLIAMENTARY REPORT 13TH JUNE, 1968